PAGAN'S
VOWS

CATHERINE JINKS

CANDLEWICK PRESS
CAMBRIDGE, MASSACHUSETTS

Copyright © 1995 by Catherine Jinks

Map illustration copyright © 2004 by Tim Stevens

First Candlewick Press edition 2004

Library of Congress Cataloging-in-Publication Data

Jinks, Catherine.
Pagan's vows / Catherine Jinks. — 1st Candlewick Press ed.
p. cm. .
Sequel to: Pagan in exile.
Sequel: Pagan's scribe.
Summary: Follows the adventures of Pagan, squire to Lord Roland,
through the years 1188 to 1189, as he accompanies his master, now
determined to be a monk, to the French monastery of St. Martin
and uncovers a dangerous blackmail plot.
ISBN 0-7636-2021-1
[1. Religious life — Fiction. 2. Monasteries — Fiction.
3. Monks — Fiction. 4. Middle Ages — Fiction. 5. France —
History — Philip II Augustus, 1180–1223 — Fiction.] I. Title.
PZ7.J5774Pag 2004
[Fic] — dc22   2004045775

2   4   6   8   10   9   7   5   3   1

Printed in the United States of America

This book was typeset in Weiss.

Candlewick Press
2067 Massachusetts Avenue
Cambridge, Massachusetts 02140

visit us at www.candlewick.com

To my dear grandmother, Beryl Dickings

The Abbey of Saint Martin

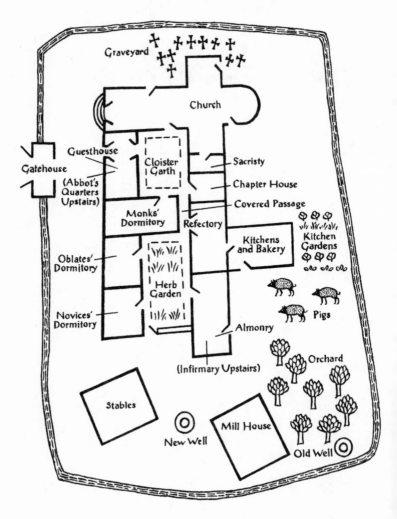

SUMMER 1188

❖

✝CHAPTER ONE✝

Monks, monks, monks. Monks everywhere, as far as the eye can see. Rows and rows of them, crammed together on their chapter-house seats like bats in a cave. Like crows around a corpse. The rustle of their black woolen sleeves as they point and nudge and whisper. The coughing and gurgling of old men with clogged lungs.

God preserve us, just look at them, will you? Talk about the blind, the halt, and the withered. This abbey must be the local dumping ground for unwanted relatives. But perhaps it's just as well. Perhaps with all these cripples around, I'll have a better chance of being accepted. They'd be mad to turn away four sound limbs and a functioning set of teeth, even if they do belong to a seventeen-year-old illegitimate Arab with a highly dubious background.

"And who is this?" Prior Guilabert peers at me with his pale, bulging eyes. I don't like the look of Guilabert. Only fools' eyes bulge like that: it's the pressure of all the air in their heads. "Is this your servant, Lord Roland?"

"This is my squire," Roland rejoins. "His name is Pagan Kidrouk."

"And he is seeking a place in this most holy foundation, as you are?"

"He is."

"As a novice?"

"Yes." Roland hesitates; glances at me; continues. "Pagan is a Christian Arab. He was born a Christian, and he grew up in a monastery in Bethlehem. Now he wants to return to the cloister."

Bethlehem! You can hear the word passing from mouth to mouth. You can hear them all fluttering with excitement.

Ho hum. Here we go again.

"Bethlehem?" Guilabert's eyeballs practically pop

out of his head and roll across the floor toward us. "You mean he's from the *Holy Land*?"

"Yes."

"And you were there, too? In Jerusalem?"

"Yes." Roland stares down at his feet. He looks so strange in this room, surrounded by all these stunted scarecrows. So very big and broad-shouldered. Straight and strong and majestic, like the pillars holding the roof up. Soft light glistening on his golden hair. "I was in Jerusalem for six years," he says, "until it fell to the Turks last summer."

"You were there as a knight of the Temple?" Guilabert's squinting at the red cross on Roland's surcoat. Amazing how white that surcoat looks, against all these black robes—especially when you consider that I haven't washed it since God created Adam. In broad daylight it's not even cream-colored anymore: it's somewhere between leper's-foot brown and fever-pus yellow. War is very hard on the color white.

"As you say, Reverend Father. I am a knight of the Temple." Roland speaks slowly and carefully. (He's rehearsed this speech several times.) "It was not—that is—I believed that the Rule of the Templars would be my path to salvation."

5

He stops, and licks his dry lips. Go on, Roland, you can do it. They're only monks, after all.

"I have long wished to serve our Lord Jesus Christ," he continues, "and in my youth spent many happy hours at the Abbey of Saint Jerome, which lies a short distance from my father's lands. You may know of Saint Jerome. You may also know that I was born on the other side of Carcassonne, in a castle some three days' ride from your own abbey. My father . . . my father is a man of war."

A brief silence as Roland swallows. Man of war? More like a murderous bloodsucking butcher. Guilabert's frowning and pulling at his pendulous upper lip; you can almost hear the passage of each word as it rolls slowly down his ear canal and drops into the well of darkness that serves him as a brain. How in God's name did a turnip like this ever get to be prior of Saint Martin's? And where, may I ask, is the Abbot? If the Abbot is as dumb as his deputy, I don't know how I'm going to survive in here.

"I know of your father, Lord Roland," Guilabert finally remarks. You can tell that he's heard all the very best stories: there's something about the way he wriggles in his chair.

Roland takes a deep breath and plows on.

"My father raised me to fight," he says, "but I was not happy in his service. I wanted to be a monk at Saint Jerome. So I applied to the Abbot, who would not admit me to his house. He said I was born to fight and that I should fight for God. He said I should go to Jerusalem, where I would be battling against the Infidel. It was there that I joined the Templars and fought against Saladin's Infidel army when it conquered the Holy Land. It was there that Pagan first entered my service."

"And now you have returned to Languedoc." (Well done, Guilabert. A brilliant deduction.) Roland nods, and gropes absent-mindedly for his sword hilt. But it isn't there anymore. So he tucks the wandering hand into his belt.

"Yes," he murmurs, "now I have returned to Languedoc. I have sheathed my sword and wish to pray in peace. I beseech you humbly, Reverend Father, to accept me as your brother in Christ."

No mention of Esclaramonde, of course. But why complicate matters? Why dwell on the fact that Roland came back to Languedoc to raise troops for the Holy Crusade, and fell in love with a heretic named Esclaramonde? Why admit that she died in a pointless, bloody skirmish on his father's lands, and that he blames himself for her death? Why point out that he's sheathed his sword in penance? It'll only upset the monks.

Guilabert's jowls wobble as he inclines his head.

"I understand your wish to serve God," he says solemnly. "But are you not serving Him with honor and courage as a knight of the Temple? A knight of the Temple is a Monk of War. Are you not dedicated to fighting the Lord's battles already? Why do you wish to abandon one holy Rule for another?"

God save us, there's a question. But Roland remains calm—at least on the outside. He doesn't even lose control of his voice.

"I no longer believe that anyone can truly serve Christ with a drawn sword," he declares firmly, whereupon Guilabert grunts. He doesn't sound too sympathetic.

"So be it," he mumbles. "But in laying down your worldly arms, Lord Roland, you will be taking up the all-powerful arms of obedience, to fight under the Lord Christ, our true king. Do you realize that?"

"I do."

"You will also surrender dominion over your own body and will, obeying with perfect submission the precepts of our most holy Father, the

8

Blessed Benedict of Sacred Memory, under whose ancient and enlightened Rule we imitate in our lives what our Lord said, namely: 'I came not to do my own will, but the will of Him who sent me.'"

(Guilabert's obviously said this a hundred times before. He recites it like the Lord's Prayer, his voice a sapless drone.)

"It is our calling and our privilege to love the Lord God with all our heart, with all our soul, with all our strength," he adds, "and in so doing to forsake all worldly things: our possessions, our low desires, our friends and family. Knowing all this, are you still steadfast of purpose?"

Roland bows. "I am," he says.

"And you, my son?" (Who, me?) "Are you willing to look within yourself, to prove yourself with all your actions, seeking not temporal recompense but the promise of God's glory?"

Um—well . . . yes. I suppose so. Yes.

"Yes."

"And will you prefer nothing to the love of Christ, struggling to attain the twelve steps of humility in the knowledge that undisciplined sons shall perish, as the Scripture testifies, and that to refuse obedience is like the crime of idolatry?"

Oh, hell. Staring up into those frog's eyes, into

that puffy, vacant face with its triple chin and sweaty brow and its network of little red veins around the nose. Perfect obedience? To this brainless tub of lard?

But I have to. I simply have to. Because it's the only way.

"I will make my submission, and prefer nothing to the love of Christ."

There, I've said it. No going back now. Glance at Roland, but he's looking at his feet again. Guilabert raises a pudgy hand and traces a cross in the air.

"Dominus sic in vobis quod aeternam vitam pervenire mereamini," he mutters. "In the name of God I welcome you, Lord Roland Roucy de Bram, and you, Pagan Kidrouk, into this noble and consecrated abbey, the Abbey of Saint Martin, so that you may follow the Rule of Saint Benedict in preparation for taking a vow of perpetual obedience, perpetual stability, and *conversio morum in perpetuum.* May the Lord's blessing be upon you in your endeavors."

A low "Amen" from the rest of the assembly. Do we have to say something now? But Guilabert presses on, as if he's in a hurry to proceed to more urgent matters.

"I will ask you both to move into the church, where you will wait until the end of chapter," he declares. "You will then receive your tonsure and your habit, and our novice-master, Clement, will take charge of you. As a novice, you are in training to be a monk. You are not permitted to leave the abbey, nor to read the lessons, nor to sing the anthems or responses. At the end of two months, the Rule will be read to you, and you will be asked if you are still steadfast of purpose. If you are, you will return to the noviciate for six more months. At the end of that time, the Rule will be read to you again. If you give the same reply, you will be tested for another four months before being received into the Order. Is that quite clear?"

Roland's shocked. I can tell by the way his lips tighten. Twelve *months*? Until we're *received*? I should have warned him.

"Quite clear, Reverend Father." (Better if I speak for both of us.) "Should we—do we go through this door here?"

"Yes. Just turn right, and that will take you past the sacristy. You'll find a door into the southern aisle of the church."

"Thank you, Reverend Father."

"Benedicite."

Come on, Roland, we're being dismissed. As I tug his sleeve he seems to snap out of it. Bows low toward the prior's chair. Turns to face the inner door.

Suddenly Guilabert opens his mouth again.

"Behold the law under which you wish to serve," he intones. "If you can observe it, enter. If you cannot, freely depart."

Freely depart? Not likely. We've come this far—no one's going to turn us back now.

CHAPTER TWO

They must be joking. I can't wear this. I'll break my neck.

"It's too big for me." Flap, flap. Just look at the sleeves, for God's sake! "How am I going to hold up my skirts if I can't find my hands?"

"Here." Roland tugs at the folds of fabric under my belt. He lifts the hemline about a finger's length, and leaves me looking pregnant. "I'm sure it won't be for long. If we cut off about this much . . ."

"But surely they could have found something my size? I know I'm small, but I'm not that small! I look like Jonah inside the whale." Or like a maggot in an ox-hide. "And what about you? Your skirts are almost up to your knees."

"Oh, Pagan, it's not that bad." He lifts an arm; the black wool ends at least a hand span above his wrist. "I'll just let the hem down."

"You?" Don't make me laugh. Since when have you ever picked up a needle, let alone threaded one? "No you won't. I'll do it."

"Pagan, you're not my squire anymore. You are my brother." (Gently.) "It's not your place to serve me, but to serve Christ."

How strange he looks without his beard. His face seems so much longer. So much softer. And that scar along his jawbone . . . I never knew he had that scar.

"You look younger without your beard." Younger and sadder, but I won't say that. "It suits you."

"And you look older without your hair," he says, smiling.

By the beard of Beelzebub. Feeling around for the bald spot on the crown of my head. There it is. My new tonsure.

"It feels so odd." Ugh! Like the top of an egg. "Does it look as odd as it feels?"

"Not at all."

"And it's cold, too. Does yours feel cold?"

"A little."

"Be honest, now. Are you sure my scalp doesn't look like a pig's rump?"

He shakes his head, still smiling. But I don't believe him. Just because Roland looks all right, it doesn't mean that I do. Roland would look all right if you rolled him in dung and dragged him through a field of nettles, face-down.

Oh, well, I don't suppose it matters. And I shouldn't be thinking about my appearance, anyway. Monks aren't supposed to be ornamental—not like the stuff in this sacristy. What a haul! The embroidered linen, the silver candlesticks, the golden vestments.

"Look at this, will you?" Picking up a candle-snuffer. "It looks like topaz."

"Put it down, Pagan."

"It's all right—I won't hurt anything."

"Please put it down."

"I wonder what those things are for?" Huge bronze tubs, lined up under the window. "Soup, do you think?"

"Pagan—"

The sudden sound of creaking hinges. Whoops! Here's the chamberlain. He stops in his tracks, throws back his head, and laughs out loud.

Yes, that's right—go on, laugh. I know we look like a couple of fools on sticks.

"Oh-ah!" he chortles. "Those aren't the best fit, are they?" He's balancing a bundle of clothes on his stomach. "You'll do yourselves an injury in those," he says. "I'd better order some new ones."

You mean you don't have any more spares? God preserve us. He dumps his bundle onto a prayer stool and extracts a long, trailing garment of black wool. His face is as red as a drunkard's nose, wide and rugged; he's practically bald, but his eyebrows make up for it. They look like a pair of drowned kittens glued to a sandstone cliff.

"This is a scapular," he explains. "You put it on over your robe. See this hole? Your head goes through there, and you attach your cowl with these strings. Then your shoulder cape goes on top. Here, I'll show you." Oh, no, please, I'll do it myself. "Hold still. That's it. There." (Suddenly smothered in black wool.) "Oh-ah. You're a dainty fellow, aren't you?"

You mean I'm a skinny little midget. Don't be shy—just say what you're thinking.

"I'll have a look in the children's wardrobe," he says. "We have oblates here as young as six years old. There might be something in their cast-offs

that you can wear until the new stuff comes in."
(Well, thanks. Thanks a lot. That really makes me
feel better.) "This is your spare pair of drawers," he
continues. "This is your spare shirt. You'll get five
pairs of socks, a pair of sheepskin gloves for winter,
and a pair of fur-lined winter boots. With everything else—like that scapular, for instance—you
get two of each. Clothes to be washed go in the
cloister chest every Thursday. Clothes to be
mended go in the chapter-house chest. If you want
your boots oiled, bring them to me. Same if you
need new drawers. If I'm not here—and I'm away
quite a lot, in the summer—you can go to Brother
Bernard, the sacristan." He moves across to a big
carved box under a pile of linen. Shoves the linen
onto the floor. Takes a key from the bunch at his
waist and fishes around in the bronze keyhole,
which guards the box like a silent sentry. At last he
flings the lid open. "Here are your combs and
knives," he says. "You'll get your stylus and writing
tablet from Brother Clement. Oh, and these are for
minor repairs." He produces two floppy leather
pouches, each containing two needles and a spool
of black thread. "Anything more serious than a
fallen hem, and you take it straight to the chapter
house. Is that clear?"

"Yes, Father."

"Yes, Father."

"Now, where did you put your old clothes? Oh. Right. I'll take care of them. Any questions?"

Yes. Is there a packhorse that comes with all this? "Please, Father—" (Hell. What's his name? Rainier?) "Please, Father Rainier, where should we put everything?"

"There's a box under each of your beds. Brother Clement will show you. Ah—and here he is now." The chamberlain grins a wide, yellow grin as he turns toward the door. "Don't laugh, Brother. I'll be ordering new robes for both of them."

Laugh? *Laugh?* I don't think Brother Clement knows the meaning of the word. Look at his face! You could sharpen flints on it. He's one of those dried-up old hunchbacks who's had the juice completely wrung out of him. Eyes like chips of ebony, mouth like a trap, two or three strands of white hair clinging to his scalp like cobwebs.

"Laughter is forbidden by the Fifty-fifth Instrument of Good Works," he says in a voice you could shave your corns with. "There should be no laughter in this abbey. Are you finished here, Brother?"

"For the moment."

"Did you describe your duties to these novices?"

"Well, no—"

"Brother Rainier is the chamberlain. A chamberlain receives and distributes all tithes, donations, and gifts. He is in charge of the abbey finances, and any buying or selling that needs to be done." (Every sentence bitten off sharply, despite the old man's general lack of teeth.) "If you would both come this way, I will take you to the novices' dormitory. At present the novices are studying Saint Benedict's Rule. Speech is permitted until the bell rings for Sext. This room is normally out of bounds to all novices."

And off he goes. What a merry old relic. I can see that we're going to have no end of jolly jokes with him. He walks quite fast, for a tottering ruin: his stick raps against the polished tiles of the church floor. A servant with a scrubbing brush scrambles out of his way as he heads for the south aisle.

"That is Brother Bernard de Moutiers," he announces, nodding at an albino who seems to be scouring the font with a piece of pigskin. "Brother Bernard is the sacristan. He looks after the fabric and contents of our church. This way, please."

Through a door and into the cloister. Covered walkways on all four sides. A patch of grass in the middle. To our right, against the church's southern wall, a series of big wooden presses. Clement points his stick at them.

"That is where the books are stored," he says crisply. "They are in the care of Brother Gerard Bonardin, our precentor." He squints around, as if looking for someone. "Brother Gerard doesn't seem to be here at the moment. But over there you can see Brother Montazin de Castronovo, our cellarer." (A tall, thin, olive-skinned man, with a hooked nose and iron-gray curls.) "Brother Montazin is responsible for the abbey diet, as well as fuel, transport, and repairs. Both the guest-master and the keeper of the refectory report to him. The guesthouse entrance is to your right: the Abbot lives upstairs when he's not away, as he is at present. Both areas are out of bounds to all novices. The building in front of you is the monks' dormitory, and the latrines are down there. This way, please."

Quick march over to the southeast corner, past crowds of chattering monks. Some of them are sharpening knives, some nursing books. One of them seems to have mislaid a forearm.

"To your left is the refectory," Clement continues, plunging into the dimness of a long, straight corridor with a vaulted roof. "Meals are served in that room to all brethren, novices, and oblates. The kitchens and bakery are on the other side of it. To your right, as I said, is the monks' dormitory; it can only be reached from the cloister. And this is the herb garden."

Emerging into another open space. It's full of mint and fennel, all laid out in tidy rows, and there's an olive tree planted against the far wall.

"The infirmary is on the top floor of the building to your left," Clement explains, waving his stick around. "Underneath it is the almonry, where the poor are received and succored. Do not tread on the plants, or you'll regret it. Some of them are very valuable. Mind the step."

He turns right and heads for a low, sheltered doorway with a saint carved on the lintel. (Saint Nicholas, to judge from the moneybags.)

"This is where the oblates sleep," he says, stopping abruptly. "On no account are you to talk to the oblates. You may exchange bows, but you must not touch them or communicate with them in any way. Nor may you sit beside an oblate in the church or in the cloister. The penalties for doing so are very, very severe."

God preserve us. Are we allowed to turn over in

21

bed at night? Or do we have to sleep face-down under a pile of gravel? Glance at Roland, but he's not looking at me. His gaze is firmly fixed on the ground.

"The last door is your door," Clement concludes. "It leads to the novices' dormitory. Notice the depiction of Saint Catherine, patron of all students, carved above it; notice that milk, rather than blood, flows from her severed head. This indicates that we shall all be nourished by the manna of wisdom. 'For wisdom is better than rubies, and all the things that may be desired are not to be compared with it.' Kindly wipe your feet before entering."

Roland goes first. He has to stoop to pass under the lintel. Me next, I suppose. Up one step—wipe my feet—through the door . . .

And into dead silence.

‡CHAPTER THREE‡

So this is the novices' dormitory. Nothing much to look at. A long, low room with beds at the far end. Cross on the wall. Chest under the window. And more castoff relatives sitting on stools.

"*Benedictus sit Dominus.*" A mumbled chorus, as they lurch to their feet: one full-grown man and five striplings. Most of the young ones look younger than I am.

"*Dominus vobiscum. Dominus vobiscum.*" Clement waves a withered claw. "Attention, please. We have two new brothers to welcome—Roland and Pagan. Roland is the son of Lord Galhard Roucy de Bram. Pagan was his squire. They have come to us from Jerusalem." (A couple of gasps, a nudge, a look. But no one has the guts to comment.) "Since most of you grew up in this abbey, you will be able to help them understand our ways, just as you have been helping Ademar." Clement points his stick at the oldest novice, who seems to have burned half his face off. He's missing one eye and quite a lot of nose; the remaining eye is wet and inflamed. He keeps his head lowered.

"Ademar is a former layman, as you are," Clement informs Roland. "He came to us about a month ago, from Castelnaudary. Beside him is Bernard, whom we call Bernard Incentor—Bernard the Tune-Setter—because of the voice with which God has blessed him. Bernard was an oblate; he entered this abbey as a little child. So did Raymond, and Gaubert, and Durand. And Amiel, of course. Sit down, Amiel. I told you not to stand unless you have to."

Amiel collapses back onto his stool, wheezing the way a wineskin does when you're trying to squeeze out the very last drop. Obviously has a bad chest, poor soul. He's just a wisp of gristle, thin and pale, with bluish lips and fingernails, and big, dark circles under his eyes. Gaubert's an even sadder case: practically a dwarf, with stunted dwarf's legs and a stump for a right hand. But he seems cheerful enough, grinning away down there.

The rest of them don't look too unhealthy, although Bernard's pimples are pretty frightening. He's the tallest of the lot, and by far the greasiest—his dung-colored hair has a lank, sticky gleam to it, as if it's been dipped in olive oil. Durand has a big belly and two chins, but he'd look all right if it weren't for his tonsure. (Some people just shouldn't wear tonsures.) Raymond's the only one who rises above the general atmosphere of desolation, thanks to his solid build and chestnut curls, but I don't like the way he's got his nose in the air. Seems to think he deserves to be congratulated for something. His face, perhaps?

"Fetch two more seats, Bernard—you know where they are." Clement lowers himself onto one of the stools, his joints cracking like nutshells. "Everybody sit. Sit. You—Pagan—what are you looking at? Look over here. I'm talking to you. Now, before proceeding, I have to point out for the benefit of newcomers that normally we would be speaking Latin, but because Ademar has no Latin, we are obliged to use the vulgar dialect of this country. Of course Latin is always to be preferred.

It is the only civilized tongue. Tell me, Roland, do you have any Latin?"

Roland hesitates, his backside poised above the stool he's just received. For a moment he's silent.

"A little," he says at last, and sits down. His face is expressionless. Watch it, Roland. There's Latin and Latin, you know. Something tells me that yours isn't the kind they use around here.

"And Pagan?" Clement turns his head. "What about you? Do you have any Latin?"

"Yes, I have."

"Verbum quid est?"

(Pardon?)

"Verbum quid est?"

Verbum quid est? What is a verb? What do you mean, "What is a verb?" Oh—wait a moment. Wait a moment, I remember now. That's from Donatus! From the *Ars grammatica*! How could I have forgotten? Donatus's *Ars grammatica*: they must have read it to us about five hundred times, back in Saint Joseph's. God, those lessons with Brother Benedict. The way he used to thrash us if we didn't get the questions right. What is a noun? What is a syllable? What is a sentence? I haven't thought about Donatus in years. . . .

"VERBUM QUID EST?"

26

Hell on a hilltop. What *is* a verb? Think, Pagan. A verb is—a verb is—

Ah, yes. A verb is a part of speech with time and person, but without case.

"*Verbum est pars orationis cum tempore et persona sine casu.*"

"Correct." Clement nods. "It is clear that you do have Latin. Where did you learn it?"

"In a monastery."

"The one in Bethlehem?"

"Yes."

A whisper from somewhere behind me. Clement raps his stick on the floor.

"Silence!" he snaps. "One more word from you, Gaubert, and it's a four-day fast. So, Pagan. You read Donatus, at this monastery?"

"Yes."

"Yes, *Master*. You must call me Master."

"Yes, Master." (God preserve us.)

"What else did you read?"

"The Rule of Saint Benedict. Master."

"What about Priscian?"

"No, Master."

"Cato? Aesop?"

"No, Master."

He grunts and turns away. What a ravening beast.

27

What a dragon. Be merciful unto me, O God, for a man would swallow me up.

"And you, Roland," he continues. "If I were to say, *Postula a me et dado tibi gentes hereditatem tuam*, what word, do you think, would govern the *me* most suitably?"

Oh, Lord. Poor Roland. This is a disaster. Roland—Roland! Look over this way! Roland! He swallows and takes a deep breath.

"The *me* . . . ?" he says in a bloodless voice. God have mercy. Just tell him, Roland. Tell him you can't read. Tell him your only Latin is the Lord's Prayer. It's not your fault that you don't have any grammar. Knights just aren't raised to read books.

"Yes, that's right. The *me*." Clement's growing impatient. "Which word governs the pronoun *me*?"

"*Deus.*"

"*Deus?*"

A snicker from Bernard. Shut up, you poisonous bed-louse. Clement's squinting at Roland as if he can't believe his eyes. "*Deus?*" he repeats. "You mean 'God'? Is that what you mean?"

Roland nods.

"But I don't understand," Clement mutters. "Why do you say that?"

"Because God governs all things."

This time Bernard laughs out loud. Right. That's it.

"Shut up!" (You pus-bag! You maggot!) Don't you dare laugh at Roland! Don't you dare!

"Silence!" *Whomp!* Clement's stick hits the floor. "Pagan! That's enough. I will not warn you again."

"But—"

"Silence!" *(Whomp!)* "Are you deaf? Did you hear me? Did I give you permission to speak? In the Rule of Saint Benedict, Pagan, the Fifty-third Instrument of Good Works is 'not to be fond of much talking.' Kindly remember that."

Oh, really? Well for your information, Needlenose, I do remember that. And I remember something else, too.

"But Master, the Eighteenth Instrument of Good Works is 'to come to the help of those in trouble.'" (So there, bog-brain.) "Roland was in trouble, and I came to his help."

Gasp. That's done it. A stifled squeak from Durand. A choking sound from Bernard.

Clement clears his throat.

"In Chapter Sixty-nine of Saint Benedict's Rule," he growls, "it states that in a monastery *no one* should presume to defend another. 'Special care must be taken that under no pretext should one monk presume to defend or uphold—'"

"Yes, but what about Chapter Seventy-two?" Courage, Pagan. Stand up and speak your mind. Looks can't kill, after all. "In Chapter Seventy-two it says: 'Let no one follow what he thinks most profitable for himself, but rather what is best for another.' What about that?"

Dead silence. Everyone seems to be holding their breath. Roland throws me one of his long, blue looks, and shakes his head a little. Clement narrows a steely pair of eyes.

"So," he says at last, very slowly and very, very quietly, "we have an orator with us. We have a master of argument. How impressive. And tell me, my young Cicero—you who are so learned in the art of discourse—tell me, what are the two kinds of argumentation, according to Boethius? What is a syllogism? What is an enthymeme? What are the five parts of rhetoric? Can you tell me this? Hmm?"

Oh, very funny. Very amusing. "No, Master."

"No? But surely you must know the thirty-two instruments of *verborum exornatio?*"

"Not personally." You big fat heap of pigs' offal. "We haven't been formally introduced."

A titter from Gaubert. Clement stands up.

"Then it's time you were," he says, and every word sounds as if he's spitting out teeth. "Come. All of you, come this way. You, too, Pagan. This is for your benefit."

What—? Who—? Where are we going? Out the door. Around the herb garden. Past the refectory. Clement's stick rapping along just ahead. Bernard, flashing me a sly little grin over his shoulder. Roland, beside me, lending support. The comforting pressure of his hand on my elbow.

Oh, Roland, I think we've made a big mistake here.

"Hurry up," Clement barks. He seems to be heading for the church. No, for the guesthouse.

No. Of course. He stops at the book presses.

"Ah, Brother Gerard. How fortunate," he observes. And there's Brother Gerard, arranging books on one of the shelves. He's a shuffling, round-shouldered, cross-looking monk, with an apple-red birthmark completely covering the left side of his face.

He frowns as he looks up.

"Brother Gerard, I have need of a book," Clement announces. "Book Two of the *De topicis differentiis*, by Boethius. Could you get it for me?"

Gerard breathes an elaborate sigh (as if to suggest that he's got enough damned work to do without other people's selfish demands), drops the stack of books he's holding, and drags over a little footstool. The way he climbs up onto it, you'd think he was scaling Mount Sinai.

"Here," he says, pulling a massive volume from the topmost shelf. "How long will you be needing it?"

"Oh—some time, I think."

"Then I'll mark you down in the register." Gerard hands the book to Clement, who staggers slightly under its weight. It's as big as a castle keep, and just as impenetrable. The spine makes a noise like a bone snapping when Clement parts the middle pages.

"Now, if I remember correctly . . . I think it's in Book Two . . . Ah, yes. Here we are." He shoves the thing under my nose. "What does this say, Pagan? Read it to us."

Oof! Talk about a solid piece of literature! One wrinkled talon, pressed against the top of the page. The script looks like the work of a blind drunkard. A blind drunkard writing with a clubfoot.

Let's see, now . . .

"Nam cum sint aliae propositiones—"

"Translate it please, Pagan. For the benefit of the others."

"Um . . . 'There are some propositions that are only known through themselves, but also have nothing more fundamental by which they are demonstrated, and these are called maximal and principal propositions.'"

(There. Happy? I hope that was fun for you, because I didn't understand a word of it.)

"The maximal proposition is the foundation of an argument," Clement declares. "It is the key to any discourse that produces belief regarding a matter that is in doubt. Can you give me an example of a maximal proposition?"

Who, me? "Um—well—no . . ."

"No? In that case, I suggest that you refrain from practicing the noble arts of rhetoric and dialectic until you have mastered their fundamentals." Tapping the book with his index finger. "Saint Augustine said: 'What man is there who can comprehend that wisdom by which God knows all things?' You should live by those holy words, Pagan. And remember: 'Even a fool, when he holdeth his peace, is counted wise.'"

Meaning that I should shut my mouth. Is that it? Well, why didn't you just say so? Why go through all this fancy drivel? It's not doing anyone any good.

"Pagan? Are you listening?" Look up, and he's baring his gums at me. (What a ghastly sight.) "I have decided to let you keep this book," he says, with a kind of vicious satisfaction. "I'm going to let you carry it around for a while, and perhaps it will help you to understand the weight of the world's knowledge. Because there are many things you have to learn, Pagan. Many, many things. Despite what you may believe."

Is that so? Well there's one thing I have learned, Master Needle-Nose. I've learned to recognize a real sepulcher-head when I see one.

And I'm looking at one right now.

‡CHAPTER FOUR‡

Look at the size of that millstone. You can hardly see from one end to the other. They must need at least a score of mules to pull that thing around. And the corn! I've never seen so much. Talk about gathering corn as the sand of the sea. Piled up as high as the roof-vaults, stacked against the walls, carried in on the backs of laboring servants.

"Here are your basins." The fish-faced servant in the green tunic starts handing around carved wooden bowls. "Your corn is on the sorting cloth. When you've filled up your basin, bring it to me."

What? What's he talking about? But of course he doesn't explain, just turns on his heel and lumbers off to the other side of the mill house. Raymond pokes me in the ribs.

"We're supposed to sort the corn," he says. "For holy wafers. Only the very best grains of corn are used to make holy wafers."

I see.

"It's one of the duties of a novice," Raymond continues, in a patronizing voice. "Don't worry, I'll show you how to do it. Just sit next to me."

He leads the way to a huge pile of corn, which someone's dumped on a gold-embroidered blanket. Chaff and straw crunch under his feet as he hurries along. The other novices follow suit, babbling away as they dust off the paving stones and sit down. Only Ademar remains silent: I don't think he's opened his mouth since yesterday morning.

"Are you sure it's safe to speak like this?" It doesn't seem possible that Clement isn't lurking outside, waiting to pounce. I can't believe that he's really in chapter with the rest of the monks. If you ask me, this whole thing is an elaborate hoax, specially designed to get us into trouble. "What about those servants? Won't they tell on us?"

Raymond laughs.

"We're allowed to talk in here," he says. "Everyone's allowed to talk in here, even during the silent times. That's because it's not the church, or the cloister, or the dormitories."

"Oh."

"You'll learn." He pats my arm. "You're just new. If there's anything you want to know, come to me. I can tell you everything."

Oh, sure. And my auntie Eleanor was the Queen of Persia. But he babbles on with unshakable confidence. (Seems to be uncommonly attached to the sound of his own voice.)

"If you want to know about the rest of us, for example, I can tell you where we all came from," he says. "I'm one of the Mir family, of Carcassonne. My father is Lord Bertrand Mir, the son of Lord Folcrand de Capendu. My father owns five mills and seven vineyards, as well as many fields and houses." (Ah. So that's why this pullet is so pleased with himself. I was beginning to wonder.) "Bernard Incentor is the son of my father's steward. Both his parents died when he was six. Gaubert is the son of the weaver Ernoul Daudet, of Cambiac. He's been here the longest—his parents dedicated him to this abbey when he was only three years old." (No need to ask why. The big surprise is that they let him live at all, poor runt.) "Amiel is the son of Roger Barravus, a doctor in Narbonne. He has twelve brothers and seven sisters, and ten of them are in the church. Durand is the son of a priest

37

from Saissac. He's a bastard, of course." (Of course.) "There are many men of noble blood in this abbey. The Abbot is one. So is the chamberlain. That's why my father chose it." Raymond turns his head, and blinks his gray eyes at me. "Who is *your* father?" he inquires.

Who is my father? That's easy. My father is the biggest heap of regurgitated pigs' tripe east of Byzantium.

"As a matter of fact, I don't know who my father is. He raped my mother. That's why she got rid of me as soon as she could."

"Oh." That's floored him. He looks away uncomfortably and falls silent.

I thought he'd never shut up.

Glance over at Roland, to see what he's doing. Seems to be getting along all right. Takes a handful of corn, picks out one grain, examines it, puts it in his bowl. Picks out another, throws it aside. Picks out a third, puts it in his bowl. Doesn't look too difficult.

"Which ones are the bad ones?" I happen to be asking Roland, but of course it's Raymond who replies. He just can't keep his nose out of a conversation.

"See how this one's black?" he says. "We don't

38

want the black ones. And see how this one's soft? The soft ones are rotten. We don't want those, either."

"What about this one?"

"That's all right. If it's a good color, and it's firm, and it isn't too small, you should put it in the bowl."

What a strange job this is. No wonder they get the novices to do it. Most monks probably can't even see the grains, let along distinguish between them. Little white hands, fluttering over the golden heap of corn. Picking at it like chickens. Black robes covered in husks and meal.

"Roland?" It's Gaubert. He has a squeaky, excited voice, much bigger than he is. Roland looks up.

"Yes?" he says, cautiously.

"Father Clement told us that you were in Jerusalem."

"Yes."

"Did you fight against the Infidels?"

"Yes."

"Did you kill any?"

Roland drops his eyes. His face hardens into its Man of Marble expression: blank, stony, forbidding. He begins to examine the corn again.

"Yes," he replies.

"How many did you kill?"

I wish they'd shut up. Dead Turks aren't exactly what Roland wants to talk about just now. But he makes a final effort.

"Some," he says at last.

"How many, though?" This time it's Bernard. His voice is thick and hoarse. "Five? Ten? A hundred?"

"He can't tell you." (Don't worry, Roland. Let me take care of this.) "He can't tell you how many, because there were too many to count."

An awestruck hiss from around the blanket. Poor things, stuck inside this strongbox all their lives; they're drooling for a good, juicy battle yarn. Even Raymond's dying to ask a question. You can tell by the way he keeps opening and shutting his mouth.

"Did he kill them with a sword?" Gaubert inquires breathlessly.

"Most of them."

"Did he ever get hurt?"

"Yes."

"Where?"

Glance at Roland. He's stubbornly working through a handful of corn, his gaze lowered. What do you want me to say, Roland? Do you want me to answer that one? If I don't, they'll probably tear me to pieces.

"In the side. He was wounded in the side."

"Ooooh . . ." A chorus of sympathetic murmurs. Amiel places his thin, bluish hand on my arm.

"What about you?" he says. "Did you fight the Infidels?"

"Yes, I did." Looking around the circle of eager faces, with their slack jaws and shining eyes. Only two of them aren't sweating with curiosity: Raymond, who looks cross, and Ademar, who doesn't seem to be here at all. His thoughts are far away, in some lightless, despairing hell of his own. His expression is enough to give you nightmares. "As a matter of fact, I even met Saladin once. No, twice."

"*Saladin?*" That really makes them sit up straight. Gaubert begins to bounce up and down like a frog in a box. (You can't help liking him.) Bernard leans forward.

"Isn't Saladin the Grand Turk?" he demands.

"Sort of. He's a sultan—"

"What's he like? Does he really have two horns?"

Horns? "No, of course not."

"Does he drink the blood of Christians?" (Amiel.) "I've heard that he drinks the blood of Christians."

"Of course he doesn't." God preserve us. Are these ever the backwoods! "Saladin is a great warrior. He may be an Infidel, but he's a noble Infidel.

When he conquered Jerusalem, he spared the lives of every single soul. And he also freed every old pauper, because they couldn't pay their ransoms. And he saved Roland, too."

"Pagan." A warning growl from Roland, which makes everybody flinch. I haven't heard him use that commander-of-the-Temple voice in a long time.

But it's too late to stop now.

"What happened?" Durand pleads. "Tell us! Tell us what happened!"

"Well . . ." Should I? Oh, all right. "If you *must* know, when Saladin conquered Jerusalem, everyone had to pay a ransom, and Roland's was fifty dinars, because he was a knight of the Temple—"

"A knight of the Temple? You didn't tell us that!"

"Well, he was. But he didn't want to pay it, because he knew that his fifty dinars would free ten women, or fifty children, and he's so noble and good that he wanted to sacrifice himself—"

"Pagan!" Another glare from Roland. What? What's the matter? You know it's true, my lord. Why shouldn't I tell them?

"Go on," says Gaubert. "What happened then? Finish the story!"

"Well, I got down on my knees and begged Saladin for Roland's life, and he freed him. I don't know why he did it, because he hates Templars, but I'll always be grateful. Always. And I say a prayer for Saladin every day." (Well, almost every day.) "He's a good man, you know. Because if it hadn't been for him, Roland wouldn't even be here."

A satisfied sigh from Gaubert, Bernard, Durand, and Amiel. Raymond, however, doesn't sigh. He snorts.

"You're lying," he says.

"I'm not lying."

"You are lying! How could an Infidel be good? Infidels are bad! Infidels are demons!" He's red in the face. "The only good Infidel is a dead Infidel!"

"I wouldn't say that exactly—"

"Oh, wouldn't you?" (What's the matter with this slug-head? Why's he splitting his seams?) "Maybe you wouldn't say it because they're your friends! Maybe *you're* an Infidel! You certainly look like one! No decent Christian would have skin that color—that dirty, Infidel color—"

Suddenly Roland gets to his feet. From down on the floor he looks as tall as a cedar of Lebanon. He moves over to where Raymond is crouching and

43

stands there, arms folded, glaring down his long de Bram nose.

"Pagan is a good Christian," he says quietly. That's all he says, but it's enough. Poor old Raymond just shrivels up like a flower in a flame. I know exactly how he feels, too; that look of Roland's would freeze the horns off a bullock. How could a half-weaned novice like Raymond hope to withstand it?

"Sorry," he mumbles as Roland turns away, and you can't help sympathizing. Poor old Raymond. There he was, top novice, brightest star, a natural leader. Then along come two war-weary veterans—seasoned travelers, Crusaders, Templars—one of them with blood as blue as the sky and a face like something on a stained-glass window. Naturally poor Raymond doesn't like all the attention we're getting.

But I have to be tolerant. I have to be nice about this sort of thing. After all, I'm a monk now.

"Come on, Raymond, let's not argue." Smile, smile. Be nice, Pagan. Think kind thoughts. "We're brothers, and we should be friends. 'Let them show brotherly charity with a chaste love.'"

"Oh, yes!" he snaps. "Oh, yes, we all know what a scholar of the Rule *you* are. But let me tell you something, Pagan." He leans into my face until I can count every scrap of salted herring wedged between his teeth. "You're never going to fit in here. Never, never, never. You think you're so smart, but you're not like us.

"You're an outsider, and you always will be."

‡CHAPTER FIVE‡

The sound of Clement snoring. But is it fake, or is it real? Surely it must be real. Surely even Clement wouldn't lie awake snoring just to lull the suspicions of some poor novice. You'd have to be crazy to do a thing like that.

Although, when you think about it . . .

Oh, come on, Pagan! Are you going to do it, or not? You can't just lie here all night dithering. Either get up and do it, or shut up and go to sleep. Those are your choices.

Raising a cautious head. Eight motionless bundles, faintly visible in the light of one flickering lamp. Pushing off my blanket. Swinging my feet to the floor. Boots or no boots? No boots, I think. It's warm enough for bare feet, and they're certainly much quieter. Padding across to Roland's bed.

He's sleeping on his back, like a statue on a tomb. Mouth closed. Legs straight. Only his steady breathing betrays the fact that he's actually alive.

One gentle touch . . .

He wakes with a start, instantly alert. Shh! It's me! Flapping my hand at him as he props himself up on one elbow, rubs his face, and raises a pair of questioning eyes.

Yes, I know it's late, but I have to see you. Come on, Roland, please. This way. Tugging at the sleeve of his crumpled robe. Beckoning. Pointing.

Slowly, clumsily, he crawls out of bed.

But can we make it to the door? That's the big question. Clement's still snoring: it sounds like someone dragging a saw through an oak beam. Someone sighs and turns over. Watch those chamber pots, Roland. We don't want to get tangled up with a used chamber pot. Guiding him between the beds, past the window, through the door, and into the garden.

It smells beautiful in the garden. Lavender and thyme. Herbal scents on the soft night air. Crickets chirping.

"Well?" Roland's voice is a barely audible hiss. "What is it? What's wrong?"

"Not here. Let's go over there, under the olive tree. It's probably safer."

The ground under the olive tree feels damp. Someone must have watered it. And there are shadows, too: shadows in the moonlight. Shadows to hide in. Branches to hide in.

"What is it?" Roland's still whispering. "What's wrong?"

"I have to talk to you."

"About what?"

About what? What do you mean, about what? "About everything. I haven't talked to you properly for three days. There are always people around."

He expels a quick, sharp sigh. "But Pagan," he says, "this is against the Rule."

"What is?"

"This is. Doing this."

"No, it isn't. Not really."

"Well, whatever it is, it's not sensible. We should go back."

"Why? What's wrong?" His face hovers above his robe, as pale as the moon. It's so hard to see in the dimness. "Don't you *want* to talk to me?"

"Oh, Pagan, of course I do. But I don't want you to get into trouble. You've already—"

"Trodden on toes? I realize that."

"You must learn to remember why we're here. We must both learn. We're not here to fight; we're here to love God."

"But I do love God." (Most of the time.) "It's just some of His monks I can't stand."

"Pagan—"

"Well, can you? Can you honestly tell me that you like Clement? Or Guilabert? Or that stupid fat monk who's always blocking doorways and slows right down whenever you want to get past?"

"But that's the whole point," he says, knitting his brows at me. "We must *learn* to love them. Like brothers."

"The way you love your brothers, you mean?"

Oops! I shouldn't have said that. And now he's thinking about Jordan. Now he's remembering how he almost killed his own brother with an iron lamp-stand. How could I have brought that up again, when we agreed to forget Roland's awful family life? Damn it, damn it, damn it!

"I'm sorry, my lord, I'm sorry. I didn't mean it." Please don't be angry, Roland. "Sometimes I just—

49

my tongue moves faster than my head. Especially when they're all so—when they—well, how were *you* supposed to know about putting your hands in your sleeves during the 'Gloria'? Nobody told you, did they? I only knew it myself because we used to do it at Saint Joseph's."

"It doesn't matter."

"But it does! It's not fair! You're only new—you can't be expected to know when to bow, and when to genuflect, and when to put your hands in your sleeves. You don't even know the psalter yet."

"Hush. Quiet, Pagan, keep it down."

"But the way he talks to you! The way he talks . . ." (That Clement. That needle-nosed maggot-bag.) "I swear, if he calls you *pauper sensu* one more time, I'm going to stick my *pes* in his festering old *faciem*."

"Pagan." Gently. "I don't care what he says. Why should I? I don't even know what it means."

"It means 'poor simpleton.' And I'll be damned if I'm going to sit there and let him call you names."

"Pagan, stop it. Listen to me." He puts his hands on my shoulders. "A poor simpleton is exactly what I am—"

"You're not! You're better than all of them! They just don't know what you've done—"

50

"The only thing I've done in my whole life is kill people."

"But you've saved them, too! You've saved more people than you've killed!"

"Let me finish, please," he says, and gives me a little shake. "Pagan, you must forget what has gone before. Do you understand? I am not a knight of the Temple now. I am the humblest servant of God in this entire abbey. I know nothing of prayer or worship. I am seeking God in the darkness, and I will take my guidance as it comes. Do you think a few harsh words are going to hurt me? You know there are things that hurt far more." He puts a hand on my head; it feels warm against my tonsure. "What does hurt me is seeing you snap at people like a chained dog, in my defense. I don't need that. Do you understand? You must forget about me, and look to yourself. You have your own path to follow. Pagan? Are you listening?"

"Yes."

"What do you say? Are you going to follow your own path?"

I'd rather follow yours. Mine will probably lead me straight into a dung pit. But I suppose, if it's really what you want—

"Oi! You, there! Who's that?"

God save us. It's the circator.

"Come here!" A voice from across the garden. "Who is it? Don't try to hide—I can see you quite clearly."

Oh, hell. Now we're caught. What are we going to do? Roland shakes off my hand and steps out of the shadows. The circator moves forward with his lantern raised.

It's Aeldred, the almoner. Reddish hair, snub nose, narrow shoulders. I've seen him in church.

"Who are you?" he says. "I don't know you."

"I am Roland Roucy de Bram. A new novice. This is Pagan Kidrouk."

"Oh, yes, of course. I remember now. The new novice."

He looks half asleep: his pale eyes are bleary, his thin hair tousled. His face is creased into lines of irritation and discontent. But I suppose the night watch must be a pretty unpleasant job, even if it only falls to you once or twice a season.

"What are you doing out here at this time of night?" he says. "You're not supposed to be here."

Roland opens his mouth to reply. Oh, no, you don't, Roland. This is where I cut in.

"He was taking me to the infirmary." Cough,

52

cough. Swaying a little. Think sick, Pagan. Think cow manure and rotten cabbage. "I'm feeling ill, Father. I think I'm going to vomit."

The almoner steps back a pace. "Is that true?" he asks Roland, eyeing me warily. Roland hesitates.

"No," he says at last.

No? *No?* Roland, what are you doing?

"Pagan is not ill," he continues. "We were just having a talk."

"You should both be in bed."

"Yes, Father."

"I'll have to report this to Brother Clement."

"Yes, Father."

Roland! In God's name, are you mad? It would have worked, I tell you! The man's half asleep!

"Well then, back to your dormitory. And don't come out again until the bell rings."

"No, Father."

"And no more talking." He puts his hand over his own mouth, a little guiltily. "I shouldn't even be talking myself. *Misereri mei, Domine.* Go in peace."

Roland! Wait! Following him to the door. Catching up on the doorstep. Grabbing his arm.

He stops, turns, shakes his head. Makes the sign for silence: forefinger on the lips, drawn up and down. Oh, you fool, you fool! Now we're going to

53

be cooked on a spit! But he won't talk. He won't even listen. He hurries back to bed and climbs under the covers.

In God's name, Roland, where do you think you are? Do you really believe that a monastery is so different from anywhere else? Do you really believe that monks don't lie? Of course they lie, when they have to. Especially when it's not going to do any harm!

By the beast of Babylon, don't you understand? No matter where you might be, you've simply got to look out for yourself.

Because no one else is going to.

‡CHAPTER SIX‡

Well, this is fun. This is a great way to spend a morning. So, Pagan, how exactly did you learn to be a monk? Oh, I spent a lot of time lying face-down on the church floor with my arms stretched out. Really? And what was that supposed to teach you? Oh, it was supposed to teach me not to sneak around the abbey at night.

But no, that's not quite true. Enforced silence was supposed to teach me not to sneak around the abbey. Lying flat on the floor was supposed to teach me not to tell falsehoods. Roland got away with a day of silence because he told the truth. But liars like me belong flat on the floor with our arms stretched out.

Anyway, I'm glad Roland isn't doing this. I'm glad he escaped this particular little lesson. After all, I was the one who dragged him outside.

Footsteps approaching. Who's this? I thought all the monks were at chapter. Turn my head and— whoops! Look out!

"Oaagh!" The feet stop, just in time. They're not monk's feet, either, because I can see brown stockings above the boots. "By the bees of Saint Ambrose! What are you doing down there?"

Craning my neck to see who it is. Yes, it's a servant. Young and grubby, with long black hair and a ripe-looking nose squashed all over his face. Blackheads the size of fortified hill-towns.

Probably safe to speak.

"I'm hugging the floor—what does it look like I'm doing?"

"Oh, I see. You're being punished."

"No, no, I enjoy it. I'm training to be a doorstep."

He snickers. His boots are covered in tallow and dried egg. They look enormous from this angle.

"How long do you have to do that?" he asks.

"Who knows? Probably until someone trips over me and breaks every bone in their body."

"I almost did. You're hard to see down there."

56

He moves away, and I can't figure out what he's doing. There's a clinking noise. And a scraping noise. And a squeaking noise like wet wool on metal. Is he cleaning something, by any chance?

"Are you cleaning something, by any chance?"

"Yes, I am." He sounds surprised. "How did you guess?"

"It isn't hard. People are always cleaning things in here. That Father Bernard must have been weaned on a pumice stone."

"Bernard Blancus?"

"Is that what you call him?"

"That's what the monks call him. I don't know what it means."

"It means he's white."

"Oh." More vigorous squeaking, as if he's rubbing something hard with a soft cloth. "It's because there are so many Bernards," he says at last. "There's the fat Bernard. He's Bernard Magnus."

"Bernard the Big."

"And then there's Bernard Surdellus. He's the one in the refectory."

"Bernard the Deaf?" I don't believe it. "You mean he's deaf, that Bernard?"

"Yes. Didn't you know?"

"No, I didn't." Thinking hard. "But then again,

we never talk in the refectory. We always use signs. So how could I possibly have known?"

He grunts and falls silent. God, I'm so bored. If this goes on for much longer, I'll end up chewing my way through the floor tiles. Come on, somebody! I've learned my lesson!

"What did you do?" The servant, still squeaking away. "I mean, what did you do wrong?"

"Nocturnal perambulation."

"What?"

"Walking around at night."

"Oh." Pause. "Which way did you go?"

"Pardon?"

"Which way did you go? Were you going through the refectory?" Shuffle, shuffle. Suddenly his feet are in front of my nose again. "Because if you're trying to get to the kitchens at night, you should never go through the refectory. You should open the gate in the herb-garden wall—it's barred from the inside—and walk all the way around. The circators never go out there."

Is that so? Well, well. "But what about the kitchen door? Surely that must be barred, too?"

"Yes. But if you knock three times, I'll let you in." He squats down and waves a damp rag smelling of rose oil in front of my face. "I'm the scullion. I sleep in the kitchens. My name is Roquefire."

Roquefire, eh? Pleased to meet you, Roquefire. "And my name is Pagan. But you'd better not stay down here, because if anyone comes in, they'll see you talking to me. And I'm not supposed to be talking."

Roquefire's knees crack as he rises. I wish I had a better view of his face. I'm not sure that I'll be able to recognize him again, if I have to do it from the toes of his boots.

"I think I've heard about you," he declares suddenly. "You're the one from Jerusalem."

"That's right."

"And you killed Saladin's uncle?"

"No." (Where the hell did that come from?) "No, I was just a squire. A Templar squire."

"But they said you were in a monastery, too."

"Yes, when I was small. Then I ran away, and learned how to fight, and joined the local garrison." How long ago that seems! Like another lifetime. "I didn't become a Templar until I was sixteen years old."

"You were smart." Roquefire's voice is gruff but wistful. "You were smart to run away. I don't understand why you changed your mind. Why do you want to be a monk, when you could be a soldier?"

Why? Because monks don't kill people. They don't kill people, and they don't have to live with it afterward. Finding the words to explain that . . . it's very difficult. And now I don't have to, because someone else has entered the church.

Rap, rap, rap. I recognize the sound. It's Clement's walking stick.

"Roquefire." Clement's voice, like the squawk of a hen. "What are you doing?"

"I'm cleaning the candelabra."

"You look as if you're sitting around on your backside, to me."

"Yes, but—"

"Get out of here. Out. 'Idleness is the enemy of the soul.' Go and do something useful."

A sullen silence, as Roquefire trudges to the door. I can understand now why he wants to be a soldier. The door creaks, and bangs. The footsteps recede.

Now it's my turn to face the Toothless Terror.

"So, Pagan. I hope you have come to repent your sins. I hope you have reflected upon the evil of falsehoods. The Scriptures say: 'Lying lips are an

60

abomination to the Lord.' In breaking with the truth, you have become an abomination. Do you realize that?"

Well, Master Needle-Nose, it takes an abomination to know an abomination. He hovers somewhere above my head, like a hawk waiting to strike. Circling . . . circling . . .

Please, God, don't let him tread on my fingers.

"In fact there are seven things that are abominations to the Lord," he continues. "The first two are a proud look and a lying tongue. You display both. It seems to me that your pride is at the root of your disobedience. You are proud of your quick wits. Proud of your little store of learning. You think that you've mastered the Rule of Saint Benedict, yet you continue to flout it! What of Chapter Seven? What of the twelve steps of humility? Tell me what the seventh step of humility is. I give you permission to speak."

"'The seventh step of humility is reached when a man not only confesses with his tongue that he is most lowly and inferior, but in his inmost heart believes so.'"

"And do *you* believe so? Of course not. Yet you have the arrogance to think that you have mastered the Rule."

"I never said—"

"Silence!" (*Wham!* He slams his stick down.) "Did I give you permission to speak? Did I? 'The ninth step of humility is reached when a monk stops his tongue from talking and, practicing silence, speaks not till a question be asked of him.' Once again you fail to abide by the Rule."

Oh, go boil your bladder, you old crow. I'm sick of this. If you're going to tread on my fingers, just do it. Anything's better than being lectured to death.

"The other novices are listening to Amiel, who is reading from the Rule." *Rap, rap. Rap, rap.* His stick strikes the floor as he circles. "Although they have heard the Rule many times, I can trust them to listen with humility, knowing that they will derive further wisdom from each holy chapter. They are not like you. You are too proud. You have a restless, frivolous mind. So I'm going to set you another task."

He stops suddenly and nudges Boethius with the end of his stick. Poor old Boethius, lying around on the church floor like a worthless Arab. But what was I supposed to do with the thing? Use it as a footstool?

"You've been carrying this book around with you for several days now," Clement adds, "yet it

62

doesn't seem to have taught you anything. That's why I'm going to ask you to read it. Get up."

Get up? Easier said than done, Master Needle-Nose. Ow! Ouch! Stiff joints, numb knees; I feel as if I've been run over by a herd of wild horses.

"What are you doing?" His voice is like someone forging nails. "Are you going to leave that book down there? Pick it up, quickly! Give it to me. If it's damaged, you'll be fasting for the rest of the summer."

He opens it and begins to flick through the heavy pages as Bernard Blancus scurries past. I wish I was going with Bernard.

"Here." Clement's found the right chapter. "This is what I want you to read. All of this, this, this, all this . . ." (Flick, flick.) ". . . and all of this down to here."

What?

"You can start reading now," he continues, "and I'm going to ask you questions about it tomorrow."

"But—"

"You will have some reading time until Sext, and another spell of reading after supper. That will be ample."

He slams the book shut and pushes it into my

hands. Oof! The size of it! The weight of it! All those hundreds and thousands of words!

"But Father—"

"No excuses." He bares his withered gums at me. (Is it a smile, or is he gnashing his tooth?) "I know that a brilliant scholar like you won't have any trouble," he says. "And if you do, remember what it tells us in Chapter Sixty-eight of Saint Benedict's Rule: 'If anything hard or impossible be enjoined on a brother, let him receive the injunctions in all obedience.'"

"But—"

"No excuses, Pagan."

‡CHAPTER SEVEN‡

Come on, Boethius, we're going for a little stroll.
Quietly, now. Quietly. Let's not disturb any of the
sleepers. Past Roland's bed. Past Raymond's. Past
the snoring Clement. All the way to the door.

Carefully pulling it open. Slowly, slowly . . . A
little creak. (Please don't wake up!) Holding my
breath as we slip through the narrow space: just
me, myself, and Boethius. It's a tight fit, but we
manage somehow.

God preserve us, I can't see a thing! Where's this
damned gate? Off to the right, somewhere. Follow
the path . . . and here it is. Groping around for the
bar, which is as big as a battering ram. By the balls
of Baal, I'm going to break my back, lifting this

thing! Damn you, Boethius, why do you have to be so big? If you were a nice quick read I wouldn't have to risk a broken back.

Dropping Boethius. Struggling with the bar as Boethius lounges there by the footpath, watching. Squeak. Scrape. Crunch. Please, God, don't let anybody hear. Laying the bar on a bed of mint, under the leaves where the circator won't see it. Picking up Boethius and squeezing through the gate.

Let's see, now. Where am I? That big, dim lump over there must be the stables. (Stay away from those.) Striking out to the left, hugging the wall, hugging Boethius, looking for the kitchens. Almost running headfirst into the almonry. God, but it's dark! I feel just like a cockroach.

If it wasn't for you, Boethius, I'd be snuggled up in bed right now. But I'm not going to let old Needle-Nose get the better of me. I'm going to learn this text off by heart, even if I have to kill myself doing it. Wait a moment. What's that up there? Some kind of light . . .

Ah, of course. That must be the infirmary window. So if I turn the next corner, and keep to the wall, I'll end up on the kitchen doorstep. Perfect. I knew I could do it. Let's just hope Roquefire isn't a heavy sleeper.

Past the almonry door, past a scented rosebush. Stubbing my toe on a rock, God curse it. And what's that noise? What's that noise up ahead? It sounds like—it sounds like—

Someone slipping out of the kitchen.

Who in the world could it be? A dim form in long skirts, holding a flickering candle. A face, bent over the candle flame: smooth, round, with small features and a high forehead.

A woman's face.

"Hoi! Woman!"

She stops. She's terrified. Is she going to faint? Yes. No. She's clutching something against her chest and whimpering like a puppy.

On second thought, she's not a woman. She's just a girl.

"Who are you?" Stepping forward to block her path. "What are you doing here? You shouldn't be here."

She shrinks back. "S-Saurimunda," she whispers.

"What?"

"Saurimunda. I am Saurimunda."

"What's that you're holding?" (Something to eat, I'll bet.) Her face crumples; she begins to cry.

"I didn't steal it," she groans. "I didn't, I didn't steal it—"

"What is it?"

"Sugar." Roquefire's voice, low and husky. He's standing just inside the kitchen door, with a lamp in his hand. "It's loaf sugar. I gave it to her."

"*You* did?" (And how, may I ask, did you get hold of that stuff? Loaf sugar is worth a king's ransom.) "Not that it's any of my business, but where the hell did it come from?"

"It's mine. I didn't steal it. It was given to me." Roquefire waves at the girl. "Go on. Get. Get out of here, quickly."

"But—"

"Get!"

She turns and flees across the kitchen gardens, heading for the eastern wall. Is there a gate in it somewhere?

"I found a hole," Roquefire mumbles. "She's small enough to squeeze through, now that I've made it a bit bigger." He looks at me sideways, his eyes glittering in the lamplight. "She comes to visit me, when she can. When I leave the red stone on the right, instead of the left."

"I see."

"She's a friendly girl. Why shouldn't I give her a bit of sugar? Especially since it's mine. It is mine, you know. The almoner gave it to me."

All right, all right, I believe you. Now let's drop the subject, shall we? There are other things I want to talk about.

"Truly, Roquefire, it's none of my business. I don't care what you do with your evenings. I came to get a lamp."

"A lamp?"

"There's something I have to read tonight."

He seems a little confused. But he nods and moves aside to let me pass. "Come in," he says softly. "Just keep it down, will you? There are cooks sleeping upstairs."

Oh, I'll be quiet—you don't have to worry about that. The kitchen smells of wood smoke and baked fish: embers glow on the hearth, and dogs snore under the table. There's a washing trough and a wicker fan, and a spice box with a lock on it. You could boil a Byzantine army in each of the cooking pots. The room is filled with brooms, buckets, bellows, skimmers, saucepan boards—everything a well-stocked kitchen should have.

Including a couple of oil lamps, tucked onto a shelf between the tongs and the saltcellar.

"You won't tell anyone, will you?" says Roquefire, as he fetches one of the lamps. "About my friend? Or the sugar? That sugar's a big secret."

"Oh, really?" How interesting. "Why?"

"Well . . . it's payment, you see. For a service."

He leans very close, and blows a cloud of garlic into my face. He doesn't look very healthy from this distance: his skin is yellow, his eyes sticky and bloodshot. There's already gray in his hair, even though he can't be more than a few years older than I am.

"But if I tell you about it, you've got to promise you won't tell anyone else," he breathes.

"That depends on what you've done." (Trying to pull away, without making it obvious.) "You didn't kill anybody, did you?"

He laughs through his nose.

"Me?" he says. "Of course not."

"Did the almoner?"

"The almoner?" His smile fades; he glares suspiciously. "Who said anything about the almoner?"

"You did. You said that he gave it to you. The sugar, I mean."

"Oh." You can practically hear his brain grinding away as he thinks. "Well," he murmurs, "it's true. The almoner gave it to me, so that I wouldn't tell anyone about his visit."

"What visit?"

70

He knits his brows, bites his lip, peers into my face. "Will you swear not to say anything about my friend?" he whispers.

"Only if you swear not to say anything about my lamp."

For some reason, this seems to reassure him. He snorts, straightens up, and thumps me on the shoulder.

"I knew you were a good fellow," he says. "I knew you weren't like those other monks. They've all got water in their veins, and feather pillows where their guts should be—"

"Yes, but what about the almoner's visit? Where did he go? You have to tell me now; you can't leave me in suspense."

"Ah. Well." He rolls his eyes and sticks his tongue in his cheek. The result is a kind of ferocious leer. "Old Father Aeldred has a lady friend. A widow."

"Really?"

"Yes. You see, every Tuesday he visits the poor, in town. To give alms. And I go with him, because someone has to protect the money. But two months ago, he began to visit a house that *wasn't* so poor." Nudge, nudge. Wink, wink. "A widow's house."

"How do you know?"

"Because I stand outside while he visits!" Another leer. "I don't see what he does, mind—I just wait on the doorstep. All I know is her name: Beatrice Mazeroles de Fanjeaux."

Well, I'll be spit-roasted. Who would ever have believed it? Aeldred the almoner! Thinking back to his pale, blinking eyes; his red, fidgety hands; his thin hair and buck teeth. "He doesn't look the type."

"Well, he is. Because he told me not to tell. And he gives me things, every time we go." Roquefire rubs his hands together, grinning. "Dried apricots. Loaf sugar. Almond paste. Syrup of ginger. Strawberry tarts."

"And you give them to Saurimunda?"

Roquefire ducks his head, still grinning. He looks at me out of the corners of his eyes. "Some of them," he says. "It keeps her happy. It keeps her coming back."

"Mmmm." I'll bet it does. Only a strawberry tart would make up for that garlic breath. "But who is she? A peasant? A beggar?"

"Oh . . ." He dismisses her with a wave of his hand. "She's just a girl. A girl from the village. She's nobody." A pause. "But if you want one yourself," he adds, with a suppressed snigger, "I can always ask—"

"No thanks." (This is getting squalid.) "I'm spending all my spare time with Boethius."

"Boethius?" He frowns. "Who's that?"

"He wrote this book." Tapping its cover. "And I've got to read it. Is there anywhere here that I can read in peace? Without a circator poking around?"

Roquefire nods violently, so violently that I'm half afraid his head's going to fall off.

"There's a place behind the stairs," he says. "It's the buttery. You can close the door, and no one will bother you."

"In locum refugii."

"What?"

"Into a place of shelter. Thanks, Roquefire. I owe you one."

"It's nothing." He winks and moves toward the staircase. "You keep your secrets; I'll keep mine."

Secrets, secrets. Always secrets. Now I really know I'm in a monastery again.

If you ask me, all monasteries are full of secrets.

‡CHAPTER EIGHT‡

What is a proposition?"

"A proposition is an expression signifying what is true or false."

"What is a question?"

"A question is a proposition brought into doubt."

"And a conclusion? What is that?"

"A conclusion is a proposition confirmed by argument."

Clement nods. Yes! Well done, Pagan! That's showing him. That's showing the shriveled old corpse. Thought you'd beat me, didn't you, Master Needle-Nose? Didn't think I'd be able to answer your questions, did you?

"'A conclusion is a proposition confirmed by argument,'" he repeats, slowly. Across the room, Raymond and the others are playing a psalm game. One of them recites the first line of a psalm, and someone else has to break in with the rest of it. Not much of a game, but it seems to keep them happy.

I just hope Roland is getting along all right.

"But what is this argument that you refer to?" Clement suddenly remarks. "Pagan? Look at me. What is an argument? Can you tell me that?"

An argument? Let's see, now. I know this. I remember reading this. Just let me think . . .

"Surely you haven't forgotten?"

No, I haven't forgotten! Just get off my back, will you? An argument is . . . an argument is . . .

"An argument is a reason producing belief regarding a matter that is in doubt."

Hah! So there. You'll have to do better than that, old man. He opens Boethius and begins to leaf through it. Hope he doesn't notice the lamp-oil that I spilled on the cover last night. Hope he doesn't notice the faint smell of baked fish.

"Here," he says, and hands the book to me. "Read the first three lines. In translation."

The first three lines? Oh—up to here, you mean.

"'Of all arguments, some are readily believable and necessary; some readily believable and not necessary; some necessary but not readily believable; and some neither readily believable nor necessary.'" (What? What is this garbage? Boethius must have had a hangover when he wrote this.) "'Something is readily believable if it seems true to everyone, or to most people, or to the wise. . . .'" (You don't say.) "'In this, the truth or falsity of the argument makes no difference, if only it has the appearance of truth.'"

Hold on. What's this? The *appearance* of truth? Look up at Clement: his expression is unreadable.

Well, I'll be damned. I'll be double damned.

"Master, you said something yesterday. You said that lying lips are an abomination to the Lord."

"Those were not my words," he replies. "Those were the words of Solomon."

"But it says here that a lie is no more than a readily believable argument!"

A pause. There's a glint in his eye, but I don't know what it means.

"And didn't the scarlet-colored beast have seven heads?" he murmurs.

Pardon?

"The Devil has many faces," he continues. "We

76

must simply learn to recognize and master each one of them."

What's he saying? What's he telling me? Peering into his wrinkled face, which is all dry and white and dusty, like a piece of chalk or a bowl of flour. But his eyes are as clear and sharp as rock crystal.

Suddenly the door opens.

"My lord!" Clement lurches to his feet. So do all the novices. They bow very low to a medium-sized, middle-aged man with salt-and-pepper hair.

Who must be the Abbot, I suppose. Abbot Anselm. Someone said he was expected this morning.

"Brother Clement . . ." He advances with outstretched arms. Kisses Clement on both cheeks. "Brother Clement, how good it is to see you. *Oleum effusum nomen tuum.*"

Clement smiles. He actually smiles! I thought he'd forgotten how.

The Abbot turns around. "Amiel," he says, in his dry, even voice, "how are you feeling? How is your chest?"

Amiel flushes. His pasty cheeks begin to glow a warm, healthy pink. "It's much better, my lord," he wheezes.

"It is? That's good. Ah, Raymond. I saw your father when I was in Carcassonne. He sends you his love." (Raymond lights up exactly like a candle.) "And here's Durand. Have you mastered the Sixty-eighth Psalm yet, Durand?"

Durand grins shyly. Bernard and Raymond laugh out loud. (It must be a standing joke.) The Abbot bends down and lays a cracked, weathered hand on Gaubert's shoulder. "You've grown," he says, whereupon Gaubert beams all over his squashed little face.

"Have I?" he stammers. "Have I really?"

"You look bigger to me. Heavier, too. Hello, Bernard. I brought back some new music for the precentor—music from the north. I can't wait to hear you sing it."

This is amazing. He really seems to know everyone. At Saint Joseph's, Abbot Daimbert wouldn't have recognized his own right foot, let alone a humble, snotty-nosed novice. Surely this can't be genuine.

"It's Ademar, isn't it?" The Abbot studies Ademar's ravaged features closely. "We've met once before, I think. How are you settling in?"

A long pause. Ademar looks down at his feet. He makes a strangled, croaking sound.

Is he crying?

"Ademar is making good progress," Clement suddenly remarks. "And here are our newest novices. Laymen, like Ademar. This is Roland Roucy de Bram—"

"De Bram!" the Abbot exclaims. His voice is sharp with interest. "But you must be Lord Galhard's son! His youngest!"

"Yes, my lord."

"I heard you went off to Jerusalem."

"Yes, my lord." Roland sounds very subdued. "But now I've come back."

"I'm glad you did. I must make some time to talk to you. So many strange things are being said about Jerusalem, although I'm sure that much of it has been distorted by distance." The Abbot's expression changes: he seems to be thinking hard. "Yes," he says pensively. "Yes . . . and with the Crusade, too. It's all very difficult. A clear account of the facts would be most useful. Most useful." All at once he brightens. He reaches up, pulls Roland's head down, and gives him the kiss of peace. "Welcome. Welcome, Roland, it is my joy and my privilege to welcome you into this brotherhood of worship. Welcome to Saint Martin's. And now—who is this?"

"This," says Clement, "is Pagan Kidrouk." (He doesn't sound too happy about it.) "Pagan arrived with Roland. He was Roland's squire. He grew up in a monastery."

The Abbot's eyes are small and brown and very alert. His face is a mass of fine lines. He looks level-headed. Experienced.

Shrewd.

"Kidrouk?" he says softly. "That's an Arab name, isn't it?" And suddenly his eyes widen. "But of course! I understand. You came with Roland. You must have been *born* in Jerusalem."

"No, my lord. In Bethlehem."

"Bethlehem!" He laughs. "Even better! I'll be expecting the very saintliest behavior from you, my child." (A snort from Clement.) "But what's this?" the Abbot continues. "What's this you're reading, Pagan?"

"Boethius, my lord. *De topicis differentiis.*"

"Boethius?" He looks at Clement in a quizzical way. "What a very surprising choice."

"'Look on every one that is proud, and bring him low,'" Clement responds obscurely. The Abbot absorbs this without comment: he just smiles a little, shakes his head, and turns back to me.

"Are you enjoying it?" he asks.

"My lord?"

"Are you enjoying the book?"

You mean I'm supposed to *enjoy* it? God help us! I have to read it, I have to memorize it, I have to drag it around like a third leg, and now I'm supposed to enjoy it as well!

"I don't know, my lord. I prefer books with battles in them."

For some reason this really tickles his fancy. He laughs his dry laugh and pats me on the elbow.

"Maybe the next one will have battles in it," he remarks. (Oh, right. And maybe my next bowel movement will turn to gold. Anything's possible.) "Welcome to Saint Martin's, Pagan. Welcome to this brotherhood of worship. I'm delighted that you've made your home with us."

You are? Honestly? But you won't be, when you hear what I've been up to. His lips feel like dead leaves, brushing against each cheekbone.

"Unfortunately I can't stay," he says, releasing my shoulders. "I've other people to visit, and there's so much work piled up in my rooms that I can hardly get through the door. But I'll see you all at Nones. And at supper, of course. I'm very happy to see you again. Very happy." He smiles at Clement. "It's good to be home."

Everyone's silent as he makes his way out. Suddenly the room seems warmer. Friendlier. Even Clement looks a little softer around the edges.

So that's Abbot Anselm. That's the man in charge. What an unspeakably wonderful stroke of luck. A good Abbot! I've never seen one before. I never would have believed that it was possible. If he stays around—if he doesn't go away too often—just think what this place will be like! It won't be like Saint Jerome's. It will be like . . . well, like the kind of place it was meant to be. The kind of place Saint Benedict would have wanted it to be.

Oh, give thanks unto the Lord, for He is good: for His mercy endureth forever.

Maybe I'm going to make it here after all.

‡CHAPTER NINE‡

This is appalling. I can't stand this. Roland doesn't belong down here, slopping around in a puddle. Just look at him! He looks like a half-drowned beggar. And he isn't doing the slightest bit of good: probably never picked up a cleaning rag in his life before. Scrubbing away at that same bit of millstone as if he wants to dig a hole in it.

Wouldn't know a mop from a donkey's buttock.

"Roland." He looks up. "That's clean now, Roland. You can move on to the next bit."

Snickers from Raymond. Shut your festering mouth, bog-brain. Say one single word and you'll be wearing your guts around your ears.

Roland smiles sheepishly.

"I wanted to make sure it was clean," he says. "If there's dirt in the corn—"

"I know. If there's dirt in the corn, there'll be dirt in the holy wafers. But if you scrub any harder, there won't be any millstone left. And without a millstone, they can't even make holy wafers. So take it easy."

He nods and returns to his slow, careful scrubbing. I hope we don't have to do this in winter. It's all right now, but what's it going to be like with cold air whistling through every crack in the mill-house walls? Sloshing around in icy water is all very well when it's sunny outside, but—

"What's wrong, Pagan?" Raymond's voice. "Feeling sorry for yourself?"

Just ignore him. He's not worth wasting breath on.

"Pagan doesn't want to do this," His Majesty continues. "Pagan thinks he's too good to scrub millstones. He thinks he's too smart—"

"All right, that's enough." Badilo pops up from behind a stack of meal bags. He's covered in meal, from head to toe. (If you took just a handful of these mill-house servants and put them in a bath together, you'd end up with enough bread dough to feed the entire abbey for a week.) "Don't you two start fighting again," he growls, "or I'll tell Father Clement."

But I didn't say a word! It was Raymond! It's always Raymond! Look at him, the viper. He sits back on his haunches and glowers at Badilo.

Who glowers right back.

"What are you doing?" Badilo demands. "Are you slacking off, boy? Get down there and scrub."

"I'm not the one slacking off!" Raymond bleats. *"Pagan's* the one slacking off."

"I am not!"

"Right. Both of you. Get up." Badilo's so broad and burly, it's impossible to argue. He folds his arms and glares. "I want you to go and refill those buckets. And if you're not friends by the time you get back, I'm going to tell Father Clement about this when he returns from chapter."

Oh, great, that's just what I need.

Raymond clenches his fists. "You wouldn't talk to me like that if my father were here, you—you servant!" he exclaims. (What a sepulcher-head.)

Badilo bares his collection of fangs and takes a menacing step forward. "Go!" he shouts.

Picking up the empty buckets, squelching into the sunshine. What a beautiful day for a journey. Warm breeze, feathery clouds, soaring swallows. A faint smell of fruit from the orchard. A stronger smell of manure from the stables. Everything absolutely as it should be, and here am I worrying about a poor little mixed-up puppy like Raymond. He's just a child, really. He doesn't know any better. Sixteen years old, and I bet he's never set foot outside this place since he was six. Of course he doesn't have a sense of proportion. Who would? I must try to be serene and concentrate on the good things.

Like this well, for instance: this well is an example to us all. Look at the steps, and the paved pathway, and the beautiful carvings in the stone. Someone put a lot of thought into this well. Someone dedicated months of his life to it, and for what purpose? Simply to glorify God.

I've got to be like the man who built this well, and make every action count.

Drawing the water, filling my buckets. Raymond stands there in silence, waiting. Watching. Phew! These buckets are heavy.

Turn back. Take a step. His foot shoots out—

Whoa! *Help!* Hit the pavement. Water splashing. Buckets rolling. Ow, my wrist!

"What's the matter?" (Raymond.) "Too heavy for you?"

Look up, and he's sneering. Keep calm, Pagan.

86

Keep very calm. This isn't a garrison guardroom. This is a monastery. Just get up, and don't raise your voice. Slowly, now. Slowly. Brush off your knees. Wipe your face. Don't lose your temper.

"Watch it, Raymond."

"Are you speaking to me?"

"I said watch it. Understand?"

Whoops! Ducking just in time. His bucket bounces off my elbow.

"How dare you speak to me like that! You miserable serf!" (He's sizzling like a goose on a spit.) "Do you think you can speak to me that way, just because Father Clement gives you your own special book to read? You filthy bastard! If you speak to me like that once more, I'll break every bone in your body."

Oh, sure. You and what reinforcements, Raymond? "Don't make me laugh. You couldn't break wind."

Whump! His other bucket flies through the air. Misses me. Hits the ground.

"Now listen, Raymond, that's stupid. That's really stupid." Trying to be calm. Trying to be sensible. "I'm a trained squire. If you do that again, you'll regret it—"

Oof! Blow to the chest! Step back—steady— digging my heels in. Ducking as he swings again.

Head down. Charge! Straight to his breastbone. *That's* done it. Feeling him yield, fall back, tumble. Kicking and rolling.

Let him roll. Jump on his back. Bend his arm . . .

"Raymond—"

"Ow! Ow!"

"Peace, Raymond. Peace. *Pax.* All right?"

He bucks like a mule. Jesus, he's solid. Jerks and thrashes. Whoops! Lost his arm. His hair! Quick! Grab his hair!

Yeowch!

Scum-bucket! Pig-swill! Bite me again and you'll lose every tooth in your head, you pustulous gumboil! *Oof!* That's it. Chop his knee—down he comes—face in the dirt—punch in the ribs. One! Two!

"Get him! Get him!" A voice nearby. Look up, and it's a stable hand. Two stable hands. Grinning and cheering and stamping their feet. "Come on! Don't stop! He's not finished yet!"

Ow! A kick—knocked back—he lunges. Slashing fingernails. Flailing arms. He grabs a rock. A rock! You maggot! You're dead, you maggot! *Hard* to his neck! *Hard* to his groin! Punch. Slam. Kick. Fight me, would you? Fight *me*, would you?

"Pagan!"

Jerked back. Struggling. Someone's arms, like iron chains around my chest. Get off! Get off me!

"Pagan! *Pagan!*" It's Roland. Roland's breath. Roland's arms. Roland's panting voice. "Stop it, Pagan, stop it!"

I'm stopping, I'm stopping. Look, see? I've stopped. Vision clearing. Who's that? Badilo? Bernard? Where did they come from?

"What are you doing?" Roland, angrily. Still holding on tight. "What do you think you're doing?"

"I didn't do anything." Gasp. Heave. "Raymond did. He started it."

"That's right," someone says. It's the older stable hand. "That big one attacked first. This little one was just defending himself—"

"Silence!" Roland thunders. (I haven't heard that voice for a long time—not since the siege of Jerusalem.) "Get back to work! All of you! Now! This instant!"

There's a general shuffling of feet. The stable hands lower their eyes and wander away. Bernard and Badilo exchange glances.

"Did you hear me? I said all of you!" Roland barks. He sets his jaw and waits as the novices follow Badilo back into the mill house.

I feel as if my ribs are going to snap.

"Roland—please—you're hurting me."

Ah! That's better. He releases his grip and drops to one knee beside Raymond's huddled form. God. Raymond. Is he all right? There's blood on the steps.

"Raymond." Roland gently touches his shoulder. "Raymond? Are you hurt?"

"Leave me alone."

A muffled voice from a hidden face. But at least he can talk. At least he's conscious. Roland frowns and leans closer.

"Where are you hurt? Tell me."

"Go away! Just go away!"

He sounds all right to me. Maybe a little embarrassed. We should probably leave him alone for a while. But Roland gets a grip on him, tries to pull him up.

"Come, Raymond, you can't stay here. You should go to the infirmary."

Even as Roland speaks, Raymond raises his head. God preserve us.

Blood everywhere.

"It's my nose . . ." he whimpers.

Oh, Lord. What a mess. But it's not my fault. Roland—please—don't look at me like that.

"It's not my fault! I told him not to! I told him I was a trained squire—"

"Go."

"But—"

"Go! You're not helping! Just go!"

"That's not fair!" (Damn you, Roland!) "What was I supposed to do, let him kick my head in?"

"Pagan—"

"I'm bleeding, too, you know! Look! Why don't you ask me if *I'm* hurt?"

"Don't be so childish."

Oh. So I'm childish, am I? Well, in that case, I might as well cut my losses. I might as well go and steal some apples or break some windows. Since they're probably going to throw me out anyway—

"Pagan!"

Footsteps, pursuing. It's Roland.

"Pagan, wait!" He catches my arm. "Stop. Please. Listen to me."

"Why should I?" Shaking him off. "Why should I, when you won't listen to me?"

"I'm sorry. I didn't mean to be so harsh. But you must learn to control yourself. You must learn, Pagan."

"What do you mean? I have been controlling myself."

91

"No. You lost your temper. I saw you." Taking my hands and squeezing them hard. Searching my face with anxious blue eyes. "Please, Pagan, you have to make this work. If you don't control yourself, you won't be able to stay here. Don't you understand? They'll expel you."

"I know."

"Then please, please, will you *stay out of trouble?*"

Oh, God, Roland, what do you think I've been trying to do? I don't go looking for trouble. It just finds me, somehow.

It's been stalking me like a panther ever since I was born.

AUTUMN 1188

❖

✝CHAPTER TEN✝

This one looks like a ginger root. Brown, twisted, covered in lumps and knobs and patches of grass. But it doesn't smell like ginger. Oh, no. It smells like . . . it smells like . . .

Ugh. I think I'm going to vomit.

Each toenail is like a slab of whalebone, and the soles are as hard as horn. But what's this? *What's this?* It's coming apart in my hand!

No. No, it isn't. Don't be a fool, Pagan—it's just dirt. Oh, give thanks unto the Lord—I thought his toe had come off.

There. That's finished. One more wipe, and on to the next. But how many more? This foot here, and the two beside it . . . that's twelve altogether.

Twelve stinking paupers' feet! For one miserable curse! It hardly seems fair. A single foot would be punishment enough. You know what they say about paupers: Their feet go down to death; their steps take hold on hell.

Whew! And it's so hot in here, too. So hot and noisy and crowded. Bedridden paupers coughing and spitting. Visiting paupers swapping names. Rush-collectors filing past, into the almoner's office with their bundles, out again with their payments of bread. Everything steamy and sweaty and smelling of underarms.

Get out of here, dog. One sniff of this foot would probably kill you.

"Is there anyone else?" Raising my voice above the chatter. "Is there anyone else for a foot bath?"

"Me!" A quavering voice, a misshapen form. He's sitting on one of the beds, dressed in a yellow almonry nightshirt. Sorry, old man.

"Not you. You live here."

"What about me?" It's a rush-collector. He's small but solid, with bow legs and a huge bushy beard. Wearing a scythe on his belt. "*I'd* like to have my feet washed."

Loud laughter from around the room. Call that a joke? I've seen funnier jokes on the back end of a bullock. And here's someone coming down the infirmary stairs: Brother Elias, with a brimming piss-pot. Coughing, of course. Every time I see that man, he's got something wrong with him. A terrible cold, or a scabby rash, or a stomach upset. Funny sort of infirmarian.

"Go on." The bearded rush-collector sticks his boot in my face. "I could do with a foot bath."

"Oh, really? How much are you willing to pay?"

More laughter. (Anyone would think that I'd said something funny.) The rush-collector slaps his leg and wanders off. The pauper at the end of the line begins to remove strips of sticky black rag from around his feet, which look soft and swollen like rotting cucumbers. Please, God, don't make him a leper. Anything but that.

Someone stops just behind me. Taps my arm. What now, for God's sake? Turning around—

And it's Saurimunda.

She must have been collecting rushes with the rest of the serfs, because there's a loaf of bread tucked under her arm. In broad daylight she looks grubby and battered. Her hands are scarred, her fingernails torn. Her skin is grayish and unhealthy. Even so, it's easy to see how young she is. She can't be more than fourteen years old.

But what's she doing? She breaks off a piece of bread and holds it out . . .

Oh, no. No.

"What's that, little brother? A love token?" (The man with the ginger-root feet.) "I think she wants to be friends with you."

No. No! I don't want it. Go away. Go! *Go!* Her face falls as I flap my hand: with a bowed head she makes her way slowly to the door, followed by a chorus of growls and lewd whistles.

"Go on, little monk, be a man."

"Give her a kiss."

"I'm willing, my lady, even if he isn't!"

Sweet saints preserve us—I've got to get out of here. Sloshing through the last pair of feet. Wrapping them in clean white rags. Rising slowly, stiff-kneed, with a crackling spine.

There, I'm done. Rejoice in the Lord, O ye righteous.

"How about our money?" Ginger Foot, again. What a thoroughly unpleasant pauper. "Where's our money?"

Money?

"What money?"

"We get a coin. One coin. We always get a coin!"

"All right, all right, I'll ask. Keep your hair on."

Picking up my bucket. (The water's almost black.) Dragging it to the door of the almoner's office. Aeldred is sitting in there on a stool, surrounded by bundles of rushes. He's passing three small loaves to a little old woman with a face like a very bad hangover.

"What is it?" he snaps.

"Please, Father, I've finished those feet. And they're asking about money."

"They'll have to wait. It hasn't arrived yet. I'll give it to them myself, when it does."

"Yes, Father. Is there anything else you want?"

"Just empty the bucket and go."

With pleasure. Back through the beds; past the staircase; past Ginger Foot. Out the rear door into fresh air and sunshine. Whew! What a relief! How lovely that rosebush smells! Feeling the breeze on my sodden skirts.

"Father Pagan . . . ?"

What—? Who—?

Oh, Lord, it's Saurimunda.

"Look here." Trying to be nice. Trying to be pleasant. "You shouldn't be talking to me. It's not allowed."

"I want to give you some bread."

"Bread?"

99

"For your kindness." She stands there with the bread in her dirty little hand. Her hair's coming out of its net: it's pale and wispy. "Roquefire told me what you did. I know you didn't tell on us."

"It was nothing."

"You're good. You're kind and gentle. I want to thank you."

"No, please. Keep it. I get enough to eat."

"Oh." She looks at the bread. (It's already a bit soiled.) Slowly, listlessly, she raises it to her mouth and bites off a mouthful. Her teeth are small and white and pretty.

Her face is pretty, too, what you can see of it.

"Listen, Saurimunda." (How shall I put this?) "Could I ask you something? Why do you visit Roquefire? I mean—no, I don't mean that—I mean, why Roquefire? Why him?"

When she smiles, a dimple appears in her left cheek.

"Because he loves me," she says.

"Oh."

"And because he's going to marry me."

Oh, sure. And John the Baptist's maiden name was Theodora Scum. "When's that going to happen?"

"I don't know. Sometime."

Some time before the Last Judgment. Poor girl. She's wrapped in a shapeless, ragged cloak, the color of manure.

"But are you really certain about this?" Carefully, so as not to offend. "Can you really be sure?"

She stares at me, round-eyed. "About what?" she says.

"About Roquefire. You could do a lot better."

"Better than what?"

"Better than Roquefire."

"How?"

How? Good question. Oh, I don't know—it's too complicated. I can't get involved in this. It's none of my business.

"Saurimunda—I'm sorry—I've got to get back. I can't stay here, or I'll be punished. So take care of yourself and—um—thanks, and—and maybe I'll see you again."

"Goodbye, Father Pagan."

"Don't call me Father. I'm not a Father." Emptying the bucket. "Go on, go home. Before somebody sees you."

Escaping back into the almonry. I hope no one heard. The last thing I need is another round of foot baths. The paupers are all still sitting there, waiting for their payout. The little old woman is shuffling along with her loaves. She snarls at me as I brush past.

Probably thinks I want to steal them.

Up to the almoner's officer. The door's half shut. Inside, Aeldred is facing Bernard Magnus, who's holding a small leather purse in his hand. (Wonder how he managed to squeeze through that door.) Bernard seems to be asking something.

"Pauperes quit sunt hodie?"

"Octo."

"Et unus denarius per unum hominem —"

"Wait!" Aeldred's voice cuts across Bernard's, sharp and furious. (He's caught sight of me.) "What do you want? What are you skulking around there for?"

"I wanted to know where to put the bucket —"

"Just leave it there! Leave it! *Faciens stultitiam —!*"

Faciens stultitiam yourself, dog-breath! Dropping the bucket with a bang. Heading for the front door. Striding into the herb garden.

Pausing halfway to the dormitory.

Wait a moment. Hold it just a moment. What's going on here?

He didn't want to be heard. He was angry at me because he didn't want anyone to hear what he was saying. But what *was* he saying?

Let me think, now. Bernard asked him how many paupers there were today. And he said eight. And Bernard said: "And one denarius for one person—"

Eight? *Eight paupers?* But I only washed twelve feet!

All right. All right, Pagan, let's look at this calmly. Twelve feet make six paupers. At one coin per pauper, that's six coins. But Aeldred asked for eight. Which means . . .

Which means that he's pocketing the other two coins.

So that's why he was angry. That's why he didn't want anyone to hear him. Anyone like me, that is: anyone who could speak Latin, and who knew how many feet had been washed.

Because he's embezzling abbey funds.

"Pagan."

Look up. It's Clement, lurking under Saint Catherine like a dog at a gate.

"What are you standing around for?" he grumbles. "I told you to come straight back. Have you finished your act of penance?"

"Yes, Master."

"In here, then. You've got work to do."

Oh, numb your gums, Clement. I'm trying to think. Think, Pagan, think! But it's impossible. He's yapping away, yap, yap, yap, and I just can't get it straight in my head.

". . . I hope this has taught you not to curse, Pagan. Remember, the Twenty-seventh Instrument of Good Works is not to swear at all, lest one forswear. Because Christ our Lord said: 'Swear not at all, neither by heaven, for it is God's throne, nor by the earth, for it is His footstool.'"

Later. I'll think about it later.

‡CHAPTER ELEVEN‡

"Deus in adjutorium meum intende . . ."

The slow chant begins. Calm and strong, deep and mellow, rising to the vaulted roof like a bird.

"Domine labia mea aperies, et os meum annuntiabit laudem tuam."

Sunlight washing through colored glass, staining the pillars blue and green and purple. Rows of motionless monks, their faces half-hidden by their cowls, their hands very pale against their ebony-black robes. Among them, Aeldred. There he is, sitting there, staring into space. Preoccupied.

"Tu mandasti, mandata tua custodiri nimis . . ."

And now the First Psalm. Carried on deep bass voices like foundation stones, with the pure, sweet sound of the children's chorus floating above. Soaring and dying and soaring again. Lifting our thoughts to heaven. Blessed art Thou, O Lord: teach me Thy statutes.

"Benedictus es, Domine, doce me justificationes tuas . . ."

But I can't concentrate on this, just now. I have to think. I really have to think. If I were Aeldred, what could I possibly be spending my embezzled money on? You can't spend it in the abbey. You can't even buy things outside the abbey and bring them back: someone would be sure to notice.

You could, however, *give* the money to someone else.

"Sederunt principes et adversum me loquebanter . . ."

That's it. That's what he's doing. He's giving the money to his widow friend, I'm sure of it. But in that case, what should I do? Should I tell someone? If the Abbot was here, I'd tell him, because it's his abbey, and I know he wouldn't like this business at all. He'd believe me, too, I know he would. Damn, damn, damn. Why's he always wandering off to councils and debates and general chapters? The bishops can't possibly need him as much as we do.

"Ambulate in dilectione . . ."

Whoops! It's a hymn. What is it? "Walk in Love?" Yes. "Walk in Love." That's all right, I know

"Walk in Love." *Sicut et Christus . . . oblationem et hostiam . . .* easy. No problem. Now, where was I? Oh, yes. Telling someone.

The prior?

Oh, Lord, not old bladder-brain. I know what he'd do. He'd just look at me with those boiled eyes and tell me to talk to Brother Clement. Too worried about quotas, and how many lambs we should be getting in tithes, and whether the serfs should be working this much or that much. I've heard him in the cloister, muttering to himself. His mind's just too small to fit one more nugget of information. Try to insert another fact in there and his skull would explode.

"Ad Dominum cum tribularer clamavi . . ."

Help! Are we on the psalms again? Glancing around, but Clement didn't see me stumble. He's too busy glaring at Roland. Poor old Roland, must have made a mistake. He's always making mistakes. I wish there were something I could do to help him. As for Clement—one of these days I'm going to shove that old man's walking stick right up his left nostril.

Look at him, standing there. Growling his way through the psalms. Talk about the beast that spake as a dragon. I couldn't possibly tell *him*: he'd bite my head off. No, I'll go to someone else. Someone like . . .

Rainier?

Oh, no. Curse it! I can't talk to him, either—he's gone off to Carcassonne to thrash out a property dispute. Oh, why does he have to be away right now? He'd be just the person. Didn't Clement say he was in charge of the abbey finances? Although, when you come to think about it, he delegates quite a lot to Bernard Magnus.

Bernard Magnus. Should I—? No, I can't talk to that quivering mound of blubber. He's the mean-minded pig who's always slowing down in corridors when you want to get past. He's the one who ate so many jam pancakes that none of the poor oblates got any. No, I can't talk to him. I couldn't be civil.

Silence falls. Are we at the lesson already? Who's reciting it today? The cellarer, Montazin. Well, that's a relief. At least it's not Bernard Blancus. Bernard's nose is always so blocked, he sounds as if he's speaking through a faceful of fish guts.

"Qui susceperit unum parvulum . . ."

Montazin's a good speaker. You need a nice powerful voice if you're going to speak. And Montazin really works at it, too. He doesn't just drone into his cowl; he throws back his head and delivers. He uses his voice like a musical instrument. You can tell that he's actually *thinking* about what he says.

You can also tell that he fancies himself a little.

"Non est voluntas apud Patrem vestrum . . ."

Wait a moment. Montazin! Of course! I can tell Montazin! He looks intelligent enough. And he also knows something about the way things work around here, being the cellarer. Oh, yes, Montazin's the one. He's bound to know what to do.

He finishes with a ringing flourish, his voice echoing around the carved-stone heads of the prophets. But now it's time for a versicle. Patience, Pagan, not much longer. And when we're done, I'll just dash across and ask Montazin if I could have a word. Let's see, now: how would I get that message across, in sign language? *I* (point at myself) *wish* (hands crossed on heart) *speak* (make a duck's beak) *you* (point at him.) *I—wish—speak—you.* That should do it.

"Kyrie eleison." It's Gerard, intoning. The *Kyrie*? Good. Joining in the chorus: *"Kyrie eleison."*

"Christe eleison."

"Christe eleison."

And now it's Guilabert's turn; he finishes up with the Lord's Prayer. Not doing it half as well as the Abbot would have done it, if he'd been available. Come on, Guilabert, hurry up, will you? I have to speak to Montazin.

"Et ne nos inducas in tentationem sed libera nos a malo. Amen."

"Amen."

Now! Leaping out of line, pushing past the tightly packed bodies. Excuse me. Excuse me, everyone. Squeezing. Wriggling. Let me through! Astonished looks from a couple of oblates. Angry looks from Elias and Aeldred.

Just you wait, Aeldred. You're going to be a lot angrier by the time I finish with you.

Catching up with Montazin. Tugging his sleeve. He turns and glances down, his eyes a clear, cold hazel.

I—wish—speak—you.

He seems to understand. His right hand makes the sign for "now." Now? Yes, please, now.

Nodding at him vigorously in agreement.

He points at the door. The northern door, not the southern door. Are we going outside, then? Into the graveyard? But I suppose we have to find somewhere to talk. We certainly can't do it in the cloister.

Across the milling heads, Montazin makes a sign to Clement. *Novice—with—me.* Clement replies by clenching his fist with the thumb raised. *I know well.* He doesn't look too happy, because he doesn't like us to talk to other monks. Whoops! Don't lose Montazin, Pagan. Scurrying after him: out of the northern transept, through the garden, into the graveyard. Trying to keep up. He has a chiseled face and elegant hands, with long, bony fingers. He stops near one of the more recent graves.

"Well?" he says. "What is it?"

"Please, Father, it's Father Aeldred."

"What about him?"

"I think he's stealing money."

Montazin's expression changes. It becomes very intent. He narrows his eyes.

"What do you mean?" he says.

"I was in the almonry, washing feet—twelve feet—when I heard Father Aeldred tell Father Bernard that there were eight paupers. So Father Bernard gave him eight coins. But there were only six paupers, which means that Father Aeldred must have kept the other two coins. He was lying, Father."

Montazin seems to be thinking. His face is unreadable.

"Brother Aeldred may have made a mistake," he says at last, very slowly. "Or you may have."

"No, Father, I don't think so. You see, I think he's visiting someone in town. A widow." (Forgive me, Roquefire, but I never made any promises.) "I think that's where the money might be going. To the woman in town."

Montazin blinks. This time he really seems startled.

"How do you know about that?" he exclaims.

"Someone told me."

"Who?"

"Well . . . if you don't mind, I can't tell you who told me. But it's true, I swear it is."

A long pause. Everything's very quiet and peaceful out here, now that the bells have stopped ringing. Just the twitter of birds, the buzzing of bees, and the faraway sound of a horse's whinny.

"Have you told anyone else about this?" Montazin suddenly inquires.

"No, Father."

"Then don't. It's a very serious thing, to accuse a monk of breaking his vows. Of course I shall look into it immediately. If it's true, Brother Aeldred will be punished. But if you've made a mistake . . ."

Another pause. Don't tell me. If I've made a mistake, you'll pour molten lead down my throat and hang me upside down from the bell tower.

"If you've made a mistake," he continues pensively, "Father Aeldred's honor would be tarnished for no good reason. That's why I want you to keep silent. Understand?"

"Yes, Father."

"Tell no one else about your suspicions. Just forget that you ever had them. If you so much as whisper a word of this to anyone else, you'll suffer for it. Is that clear?"

"Yes, Father." (In God's name! I just said so, didn't I? What's the matter with you?)

"And I don't want you poking around in Father Aeldred's affairs anymore." His voice is hard and imperious. "You're not qualified to do so. I'll look into this, and if there's any problem, I'll take care of it."

"But what about the Abbot?"

"The Abbot?"

"You're going to tell him, aren't you? When he gets back?"

"Of course I will. Now off you go to Brother

Clement. And don't mention Brother Aeldred. Think of another story."

Looking up into his face. It isn't anxious. It isn't upset. It's just very, very cold.

This is most unusual.

"You mean I should lie, Father?"

"No, of course not," he snaps. "Just tell him you had to see me on private business."

Private business? Oh, sure. "Perhaps I should say that I was lodging a complaint about last night's stuffed olives."

"Mmm," he grunts. But he's not really listening. His thoughts are far away. "Go on," he says. "And remember what I told you. *Complete silence.*"

Complete silence. Well, all right. If you say so, Father, you're the expert. I'm just a scum-sucking novice with a bad reputation.

The last thing I want to do is get into trouble.

‡CHAPTER TWELVE‡

So now I know what the big, bronze tubs are for. They're not for soup. They're for washing altar linen.

Bernard Blancus demonstrates, using a long wooden stick. First you fish around in the tub of cold water and drag out a soggy white corporal (which has been soaking there all night.) Then you carry it, limp and dripping, to the next tub. *Splat!* In it goes. Bernard Blancus makes a fist with his right hand and rubs it against his left. What's that supposed to mean?

"Lye," mouths Durand. (He must have seen the lost look on my face.) Ah, I see. So it's a tub full of lye.

Now you wait while Bernard passes the corporal to Roquefire, who gives it a good pounding with his beater. He doesn't look too happy: he's all bruised around the jaw. But he's certainly energetic when it comes to cleaning linen. He slaps it onto his washboard and pummels it and rubs it and wrings it out and pummels it again. Finally he flings it into the last tub, which—according to Bernard Blancus—is full of cornflour solution. (He makes the sign for corn; the sign for flour.) I wonder what the cornflour does. Stiffens things, I suppose. Next you push your linen around the tub for a while, before scooping it up and carrying it, with great care, out of the sacristy.

Which Bernard Blancus proceeds to do.

Everyone looks at each other. Should we go with him? Perhaps we should. So all the novices file into the transept and follow the trail of wet drips around the corner. Through the presbytery door. Into the bare, open space behind the chapter house.

Here Bernard Blancus has arranged several laundry lines.

"You bust hag it od here," he snuffles. (Translation: You must hang it on here.) Well, that's pretty straightforward. I'm sure we can all manage that.

116

He places his corporal over one of the lines, fastens it with a cheap wooden peg, and bustles back into the presbytery. He makes an odd sound as he walks: it must be all the pegs he's carrying in that bag around his waist.

Everyone slouches after him.

"Don't forget to watch Pagan," Raymond mutters just before he crosses the threshold. "Pagan knows all about laundry. He's an expert."

Meaning that I've spent most of my humble life washing dirty clothes. Ha, ha. Very amusing. But there isn't enough time to respond, because now we're in the church again, and we're not allowed to talk in here.

Bernard Blancus hands out wooden sticks as we enter the sacristy. One for Raymond. One for Gaubert. One for Amiel. Raymond heads for the cold-water tub and pulls out a piece of linen that looks like an altar frontal. Why does he always have to look so smug when he does things? Anyone would think he's defeated an entire Infidel army with a slice of cheese tart.

If I were Raymond, and I'd been soundly thrashed by an illegitimate Arab at least a hand span shorter than me, I'd be a little more self-effacing.

A nudge from Roland. What? Oh, my stick. Thanks. Moving up to the first tub. Climbing onto the stool. Peering in at the stew of wet linen. Let's see, now. I like the look of that piece—it seems nice and small.

Dragging it out on the end of my stick. Yes, it's small, all right. I can't even see what it is. A pall, perhaps? Climbing down, and heading for the lye tub. Roquefire is waiting there with his beater and washboard.

"Hello, Roquefire." (Very quietly, out of the corner of my mouth.) "What happened to your face?"

He glares at me as I drop my linen into the lye. He looks positively ferocious.

"I'm not allowed to talk to you," he whispers.

"What? What do you mean? Who said?"

"Father Montazin."

"The *cellarer*?"

"It was a secret! All that stuff about the widow— I told you it was a secret!" Retrieving my linen from the tub, he slaps it onto his washboard and begins to beat away like a blacksmith. "Father Montazin says that if I talk to you again, I won't be allowed to go to Carcassonne with the almoner anymore. So just leave me alone!"

"But—"

"Get lost!" he hisses. "And if you come near the kitchens again, I'll call the circator!"

He flings the wet linen into my face and turns to help Roland. Glance over at Bernard Blancus. Did he see any of that? But he's too busy handing out clothes pegs to Durand and Amiel. Oh, please, please let him stay in here. I need time to think. I need time to tell Roland. . . .

Collecting my peg. Carrying my linen to the laundry line. Passing Raymond on the way: he's already hung out his altar cloth and is returning to pick up something else.

He pokes out his tongue at me.

By the breath of Hell. Just grow up, will you? Reaching the line, finding a space. Fumbling with my soggy white square. Come on, Roland, get a move on. Where are you?

At last he emerges from the presbytery door, bearing something long and purple.

"Roland!"

He pauses. Blinks. Looks around. Over here, Roland, hurry! Grabbing his sleeve as he approaches.

"I've got to talk to you."

"Pagan—"

"Listen to me! Just listen!" Lowering my voice, so that Durand doesn't hear. "Please, it's important."

He frowns down his long nose. "What's wrong?" he says. "Are you ill?"

"No, I—I just found something out. . . ." God, where shall I begin? "I didn't tell you this before, because I knew you wouldn't like it, but—well— several weeks ago I was told something. About the almoner." Take a deep breath, Pagan. Slow down. "I was told he was visiting a widow, in Carcassonne."

Pause for his response. But there's nothing. Just a stunned silence.

Good.

"I kept it a secret, because I didn't want to make trouble. You told me not to make trouble." (I'm trying to be good, Roland, really I am.) "But then last week, when I was in the almonry, I found out something else. I found out that Aeldred was stealing alms. So I went to the cellarer—"

"Pagan—"

"Wait. Let me finish. I went to the cellarer and told him everything. And he told me that he'd look into it. He also told me to keep my mouth shut." (God, God, God, no wonder!) "And I said I would. But it's been a week now, and the almoner's still the almoner, and he hasn't been flogged, or chastised, or given any other kind of penance, and that would be all right—I could have made a mistake—except now I've heard something very strange from Roquefire."

"Roquefire?" Roland sounds bewildered.

"The servant. In the sacristy. He's the one who told me about Aeldred in the first place, because he goes with him into town every week. And now the *cellarer* has told him never to talk to me again, or he won't be allowed to go on those trips anymore!"

Waiting for a comment. Well? *Well?* He puts his hand to his temple and closes his eyes. Oh, come on, Roland!

"Don't you see? It means that the cellarer is probably involved!"

"Pagan—"

"Don't you see it makes sense? Why would he let the almoner keep doing what he's been doing? Unless he approves of it." Oh, Lord, what a cesspool. And who else is involved? That's what I want to know. Rainier? Gerard? Guilabert? "If only the Abbot were here! He'd deal with it. He's the only one I trust. He's the only one who'd believe me. . . ." Looking at Roland. He's standing there with his head bowed, a blank expression on his face. "What should I do, my lord? What do you think I should do?"

Pause.

"I don't know," he replies.

Oh, come on, Roland, you can do better than that. "But you must have some idea. Some kind of suggestion—"

"Wait for the Abbot." His voice is dull and tired. "If you trust him, wait for him."

"Yes, but it's going to be at least a month. We can't just sit here and let those hypocrites steal money from the poor—"

"Pagan, please. Don't talk like that. You may be wrong. These are only suspicions."

Suspicions?! Well, thanks a lot! "My lord, I know a racket when I see one. I used to be part of one, in Jerusalem. Remember? When I used to collect protection money for the viscount—"

"Yes, I know you lived in a sewer, Pagan. Maybe that's why you see evil wherever you go."

What?

Oh, Roland. How could you? That's just—that's just—

"That's a terrible thing to say."

"Forgive me—"

"How can you say that? It's not fair! I don't go looking for this stuff—I just find it!"

"Yes, but why must it always be you, Pagan?

122

Why?" (What's the matter with him? He looks so miserable.) "I came here to look for refuge. This is supposed to be our path. . . ." His voice becomes more and more incoherent. "I don't have any authority. . . . I can't do anything. . . ."

"You don't have to do anything. I will."

"But you're just a novice! Why should *you* be the one? Please, Pagan, must you pursue this? Can't you leave these matters to the people who should be concerned with them?"

I don't believe it. This can't be Roland talking. His face is pale; he's breathing heavily. Something's hurt him deep inside.

"What are you afraid of, my lord?"

"Don't call me that! I'm not your lord any longer. We are both subject to the monks of this abbey—"

"What are you afraid of, my lord?"

"I'm afraid that you will be expelled," he says, and lifts his gaze to the sky. "You know how hard it was to find this haven. If you should be expelled . . ."

"I won't be expelled."

He shakes his head sadly. "We came here to find peace," he murmurs. "Peace, not war. If your eyes were fixed on the face of God—if your soul were striving to see the Good of all good—you would

123

be blind to these wretched conspiracies. You should be looking to the heavens, not to the earth."

A cold fist closing around my stomach. Around my heart. "What are you saying?" (It's hard to form the words.) "Are you saying that I don't belong in this abbey?"

"I'm saying that you should be careful. Please. I can't protect you here—"

The sudden sound of clapping. It's Bernard Blancus, hovering at the presbytery door. He looks cross.

"Whad are you doig?" he exclaims. "Cub bag idside ad once. There's bore worg to be dud."

Yes, well. I'm not absolutely sure, but that *sounded* like a summons. Something about more work to be done? As Bernard retreats back into the church, Roland stoops and puts his mouth to my ear.

"Please wait," he whispers. "Fix your eyes on God, and wait until the Abbot returns. I don't want you to run any risks. Please, Pagan."

Hmmm.

‡CHAPTER THIRTEEN‡

Clement shuts his eyes for a moment, thinking hard. *"Ut navem, ut aedicium idem destruit facillime qui construxit,"* he finally declares, *"sic hominem eadem optime quae conglutinavit natura dissolvit."*

And he sits there, waiting, like a frog on a rock. Waiting for me to answer. Come on, Pagan, think. Think hard. If *destruit* means destroy . . . aha! Got it.

"'As the builder most readily destroys the house that he has built, so nature is the agent best fitted to give dissolution to man.'"

Clement nods. Not a word of praise, naturally. No "Good" or "Excellent" or "Well done." I'm more likely to see an apple core in full armor than I am to hear a compliment issue from the mouth of Brother Clement.

"Now," he says, "is that particular sentence a syllogism, an induction, an enthymeme, or an example?"

Hmm. Well it's not a syllogism. An example? No . . .

Oh, of course.

"It's an induction."

"Why do you say that?"

"Because induction is an argument by means of which there is progression from particulars to universals."

He nods. Hurrah! I knew it.

"And where," he continues, "can we find the proposition, in this induction?"

"In the first clause."

"And is it an affirmative or a negative proposition?"

"It's—it's—" (Come on, Pagan, what is it?) "It's affirmative!"

"Predicative or conditional?"

By the bones of St. Barnabas. "Oh—er—um—predicative?"

"Universal, particular, indefinite, or singular?"

Oh, God. *I* don't know! My head's spinning. I've lost track. . . .

"Hurry up, boy. What's the delay? This is as simple as bread and cheese." Clement's voice is like a wasp: buzzing, circling, waiting to sting. "What's happened to your intellect? Come on, wake up! Is this the best you can do? I thought you were a master of dialectic—"

Suddenly the door opens. Yes! Praise God! It's the porter.

"Well?" Clement frowns at him. *"Quid?"*

"Veni, Frater."

"Nunc?"

"Nunc."

Painfully, Clement struggles to his feet. All this wet weather seems to have slowed him down: his knees are stiff, his knuckles shiny and swollen. He grimaces every time he has to bend over.

"I shan't be long," he says, and glares at me. "When I come back, I'll be expecting three predicative syllogisms. All in the first mood of the first form. As for the rest of you . . ." (His gaze sweeps across the huddle of novices at the other end of the dormitory.) "You may continue with your reading."

Tap-tap, tap-tap, tap-tap. And out he goes, leaning heavily on his walking stick. *Clunk!* The door swings shut behind his stooping shoulders.

I wonder what's happened.

"I bet it's him again." (Raymond, quietly.) "I bet he's done something wrong."

"Who?" says Bernard. "You mean Pagan?"

"Who else?"

God preserve us. I've had enough of this. Swinging around on my stool to confront the miserable threadworm. "Are you addressing me, Raymond?"

"I wouldn't stoop so low."

"Then keep your voice down."

"Or what?"

"Oh, please," Amiel cries, "please don't start!"

Roland is already on his feet, grim and glowering. "Enough," he says. "Enough of this. Pagan, we are not here to fight."

"Tell that to Raymond!"

"I am. And I'm also telling you." His coldest, deadliest Templar voice. "If you cannot speak to each other in a civil fashion, then you shouldn't speak at all."

"Says who?" Raymond snaps. Bad idea, Raymond. He flinches as Roland skewers him with a perfectly expressionless, sky-blue gaze.

There's a long silence.

"I think we should return to our reading," Roland says at last. And he sits down again. "Amiel?"

Amiel fumbles with the psalter in his lap. Opening it, he begins to read aloud. *"Mihi,"* he quavers, *"autem nimis honorati sunt a mici tui . . ."*

Oh, Lord, how tired I am. Please, God, don't let Clement return. Let the east wind carrieth him away. If I see one more predicative proposition, I'm going to throttle it with a bookmark and stuff it down the nearest latrine. Damn you, Boethius, I'd kill you if you weren't dead already.

Syllogisms. Syllogisms. The first mood of the first form . . .

But it's no good: I've run out of time. Because there he is on the threshold, back to poison my existence. Old Needle-Nose.

"Pagan?" he growls.

"Yes, Master."

"What is the Sixty-fourth Instrument of Good Works?"

(The Sixty-fourth?) "It's . . . it's to love chastity."

"Correct. And do you know what that means?"

Uh-oh. Something tells me I'm in trouble.

"Yes, Master, I think so."

"What does it mean?"

Glance at Roland. No help there. Clement lowers his head like a bull.

Gulp.

"It means—I suppose it means keeping your penis to yourself."

A snort from Bernard. Clement slams his stick down hard against the floor.

"It means *keeping away from women!*"

"Yes, Master."

"'More bitter than death is the woman, whose heart is snares and nets.' Her house is the way to hell, Pagan. Has no one ever told you that?"

Only about five hundred and eighty-seven times. Clement begins to cripple his way across the room, breathing heavily. He looks ready to kill.

"'Whoso pleaseth God shall escape from her,'" he splutters, "'but the sinner shall be taken by her.' You are a novice, Pagan. Novices do not associate with members of the opposite sex!"

"But I haven't—"

"There is a woman at the gates! She has been asking for you repeatedly!"

Oh, Lord. Saurimunda.

"You know her, don't you?" (Peering into my face.) *Don't you?*

"Yes."

"Is she a relative?"

"Well, no—"

"Then you must forsake her entirely. *Entirely,*" he exclaims, leaning closer. "Pagan? Do you hear?"

I'd have to be deaf if I didn't. "Yes, Master, I hear." (Wiping his spit off my forehead.)

"All of you, listen to me." He shuffles over to his stool and lowers himself onto it. He looks worn out. "I want you to remember the words of Saint Paul the Apostle, who said: 'It is good for a man not to touch a woman.' A woman takes possession of a man's precious soul, and the strongest men are ruined by her. . . ."

Blah, blah, blah. Same old stuff. Anyone would think that Saurimunda had venomous snakes growing out of her nostrils. What the hell does he think she wants—my bowels for breakfast? Although, come to think of it, what *does* she want? I told her I'm not allowed to speak to her. Unless . . . perhaps it's something really important.

Perhaps it's something to do with Roquefire.

"Chastity is more than just forswearing women."

(Clement, still droning on.) "Chastity is purity. Purity is the Twenty-first Instrument; it is preferring nothing to the love of Christ. Impure love summons the soul to lust after earthly things, whether they be women or riches or fame. Saint Augustine said: 'Cleanse therefore thy love. Turn the waters flowing into the drain into the garden.' For the soul that is bound by the love of the earth has birdlime on its wings, and cannot rise up . . ."

Maybe I should go and see her. Maybe I should slip out tonight. If she's so desperate to talk to me, she might wait by the hole in the wall. Or she might hang around the front gate, in case I make an appearance. It's not much of a chance, but—

Wait! I know! That rock! The red rock. What did Roquefire say? Something about leaving it on the right, instead of the left? That's it. That's what I'll do. A signal. If I can just slip out before sunset, and find the right stone . . .

But then she'll think it's Roquefire. She'll think it's his signal, and she'll go straight to the kitchen. Damn, damn, damn, that won't work.

No, I'll take a chance that she's waiting. I'll see if she's there, and if she's not, well, too bad. I'll have done my best.

Let's just hope that she's worth all this trouble.

"Pagan?" (Uh-oh.) "Are you listening to me?"

"Yes, Master."

"What did I just tell you?"

"Um—" Ugh. Help. "It was about chastity."

"What about chastity?"

"Um . . ."

Smirks from Raymond. That's right, bladder-brain, laugh. See if I care. Clement shakes his head in disgust.

"You were not listening at all," he says. "You are lying. Bread and water for you tonight, Pagan. 'A man's belly shall be satisfied with the fruit of his mouth.' You should learn to tell the truth, my friend, for he that covereth his sins shall not prosper, but whoso confesseth and forsaketh them shall have mercy."

Oh, sure. Tell that to Aeldred. Tell that to Montazin, and every other hypocrite who's involved in his nasty little conspiracy of silence. Talk about whited sepulchers. Talk about blind guides who strain at a gnat and swallow a camel.

Let me tell you something, Master Clement. He that walketh uprightly walketh surely, but he that perverteth his ways shall be known.

So if you've been perverting your ways, old man, you'd better watch it. Because I'm onto you now.

‡CHAPTER FOURTEEN‡

No moon tonight; it's as dark as the Queen of Sheba's armpit. How am I ever going to find that hole in the wall? How am I ever going to get through the vegetable garden without leaving a trail of squashed leeks and trampled strawberry plants behind me?

Maybe this wasn't such a good idea.

Feeling my way past the stables, around the almonry, splashing through icy-cold puddles. Praise God that it's stopped raining. I'd be stuck if it hadn't. Imagine what Clement would say if I climbed out of bed in a sopping-wet robe tomorrow. "Bladder problems, Pagan?" It doesn't bear thinking of.

Ah! And here's the kitchen. Just don't fall over that doorstep, whatever you do. Taking it slowly. What's this? A bucket? Watch the bucket. Groping . . . groping . . .

"Ouch!" Damn it! Who left this shovel here? A person could break every bone in his body! God, I hope no one inside heard that. Waiting. Waiting. Holding my breath.

Praying that the cooks are heavy sleepers.

"Pagan?"

A whisper in the dark. A rustling sound. Who—? Where—?

Someone sniffing close by.

"Is that you, Pagan?"

"Saurimunda?"

"Oh, it is you!" Her hiss turns into a wobbly squeak. "I thought you were one of the others—"

"Shh!" Groping around to find her. Here she is. Smooth skin—a little wet knob—

Whoops! It's her face.

"We can't stay here." Leaning close to where her ear should be. (She smells of damp earth.) "Show me where the hole is. In the wall."

Saurimunda touches my chest, my arm, my wrist,

135

and finally my hand. Her fingers are small and cold and slippery. She gives a slight tug as she begins to move.

Her feet make almost no sound on the sodden pathway.

Please, God, don't let anyone find us. If I'm found with a girl, I can kiss my guts goodbye. Stumbling along in her wake, between dripping beanstalks, ghostly turnip greens, makeshift wooden fences. Under a low branch. Around a puddle.

This girl must have eyes like an owl's.

And suddenly, the wall. Looming dense and dark against a paler sky. Ow! Ouch! Spiny bushes growing along its base.

"Here," she whispers, "here it is."

Where? I can't see a thing. She pulls me down and guides my hand to a small pile of rubble.

"Here," she says. "It's the hole. Right here."

"Would I fit through, do you think?"

"Maybe." She sounds dubious. "I don't know."

Well, then, perhaps I'd better not try. The last thing I need is to get stuck in a hole.

"It doesn't matter. We can talk here." Trying to retrieve my hand, but she won't let go. She just clutches it more tightly and carries it to her lips.

Cold, fervent kisses.

"Don't." (Let go!) "Please—don't do that."

"Oh, Father. Oh, Father." She's sobbing and sniffing. "Thank you so much—"

"Let go, will you? Please. And don't call me Father."

"But you came, you came! I never thought you would. I never, never thought you would. . . ."

"Then why were you waiting?"

"I was waiting for R-Roquefire." Her voice wobbles tearfully. "I thought he might—I thought—I've been waiting and waiting—"

Oh, Lord. Patting her on the back as she groans and gulps and heaves, poor thing. Waiting for Roquefire? Don't tell me it's a lovers' tiff.

"So what's the problem? You'd better tell me—I can't stay long, you know."

"It's Roque—Roque—"

"Roquefire? What about him?"

"He won't see me!" she wails. (Hush, girl, keep it down.) "He won't talk to me anymore!"

"What do you mean, he won't talk to you?"

"It's been two weeks. . . . He hasn't touched the stone . . . won't open the door. . . . I can't get in, without people seeing. . . ." Her voice is soggy and incoherent. "When I ask at the gate, he won't come out. They say he's not allowed to. . . ."

137

Hmmm.

"He said . . ." (Hiccup.) "He said he was going to m-marry me!"

"Shhh, calm down." Squeezing her hand. "Don't cry, there's no need to cry."

"But what did I do? I d-didn't do anything. . . ."

"Of course you didn't." The question is, who did? A monk? A cook? Perhaps Montazin found out and had a quiet word with Roquefire.

Or perhaps Roquefire has found someone more to his taste. Anything's possible.

"I'm very sorry, Saurimunda, but I don't quite see what you want. From me, that is."

A pause. You can hear her gulping away in the darkness, trying to regain some measure of self-control. At last she says, "I just want to see him. I want to ask him why he's doing this."

"Yes, but—"

"All I need is to get in. Through one of the doors." She strokes my hand as if it were a dog. "*You* could let me in," she adds shyly.

"Oh, no." Wrenching my hand away. "No."

"But he won't come out! I can't get in to see him, and he won't come out! He never comes out!"

"Yes, he does." Suddenly remembering. "He leaves the abbey grounds every Tuesday."

"With a monk," she complains. "There's always a monk with him—"

"Be quiet. Just listen to me." Trying to think. What was the name? Mazzi—? No. Mazeroles? That's it. That's the one. "Now look, Saurimunda. If I tell you something, will you promise not to tell anyone else?"

"Oh," she says breathlessly, "I promise."

"Do you swear by the Holy Virgin?"

"I swear. I swear by the Holy Virgin."

"All right. Well, it just so happens that every Tuesday, Roquefire goes with the almoner into Carcassonne, where they visit a house belonging to a widow called Beatrice Mazeroles de Fanjeaux. But Roquefire doesn't go into the house. He waits outside for the almoner." Peering into the shadows, I wish I could see her face. "Now, Carcassonne isn't even a day's walk from this abbey. So if you can somehow get to Carcassonne and find the house of Beatrice Mazeroles de Fanjeaux—"

"I can wait for them there!" she squeals, and grabs my hand again. More passionate kisses. "Thank you! Oh, thank you! You are my friend! You are my dear Father—"

"Will you stop doing that!" Trying to shake her off. God preserve us, it's driving me mad. "And for

139

the last time, I'm not a father. I'm just a novice. You can call me Pagan."

"Pagan," she murmurs. "Heaven bless you, Pagan. You are so good. You are my angel of the Lord—"

"Don't be ridiculous." God, this is excruciating. "And don't thank me. I don't even know where the house is. Do you?"

"Oh, yes." Her voice is high and hopeful, but still a little unsteady. "Lord Gilles owns a vineyard where my father works."

"Lord Gilles?"

"Lord Gilles de Castronovo. He's the father of Lady Beatrice."

"Castronovo?"

"What's wrong?" A frightened squeak. "What did I say?"

"Nothing. Nothing, it's—it's all right. Really."

Hell's teeth! Castronovo! That's Montazin's name! And if Beatrice is a Castronovo . . .

Then I've found the connection.

"What else do you know about Lady Beatrice?" Stay calm, Pagan. Don't frighten the poor girl. "Does she have any brothers?"

"No."

"What about cousins?"

140

"I don't know." (Snuffle.) "I don't know anything."

"It doesn't matter. Really. You've been a great help."

Yes, indeed, a great help. Well that's it, then. Either Aeldred is in love with Montazin's relative—and Montazin approves—or Montazin is somehow making Aeldred visit her. Perhaps to give her alms money. But if that's the case, why is Aeldred involved? He can't be related. He doesn't even come from this part of the world: somebody said he was born in Normandy. Or was it Burgundy? No matter. The point is, why would he be helping Montazin? Friendship? Money? Fear? Blackmail? If only I could find out. If only I knew what was going on.

"Listen, Saurimunda." Groping about. Finding her hand. "Could you do something for me?"

"What?" She sounds nervous.

"It won't be difficult. I want to write to this widow, Lady Beatrice, but I don't want anyone to know what I'm doing. So I need you to take my letter to Carcassonne. Will you do that?"

"Ohh . . ." She expels a long, awestruck sigh. "You mean a *letter*? To read?"

"That's it."

"You've written one? A real one?"

"Not yet, but I will. Tomorrow." Let's think, now. Think hard. What's the best course of action? "If I was to leave it right here, under a stone, could you pick it up?"

"Yes. Oh, yes."

"And you could give it to someone at the widow's house?"

"I would do anything for you, Pagan. You are my good angel—"

"Yes, yes, all right, I know." (Give it a rest, will you?) "But Saurimunda, listen to me. You mustn't say who wrote it. Is that clear? *Do not say who wrote it.*"

"No, Pagan, I won't."

"Good." Dropping her hand. Rising to my feet. I can hear the swish of her skirts as she moves. "And now I'm leaving; I've been here much too long already. Can you show me how to get back to the kitchen?"

"Yes, of course. Thank you. Thank you, Pagan—"

"Don't mention it."

She grabs my sleeve and makes for the low black bulk of Saint Martin's. Wet leaves slapping at my ankles. Squelch, squelch, squelch through a patch of mud. I hope it doesn't stick to my boots; the Toothless Terror would be sure to notice. But even if he does, so what? I'm still glad I came. It's given me a chance to stir the pot a little. Just to see what rises to the surface.

Who knows? I may be able to scare this widow off. I may be able to plug the leak in the almonry.

"Here." Saurimunda stops and drags on my arm until my right ear's almost level with her mouth. "Here it is," she whispers. "God bless you, Pagan." Suddenly, a stranglehold. Help! What's she doing? Fierce hug—smacking kiss—and she disappears into the darkness.

God preserve us. God preserve us, that was . . . that was a shock. Hands shaking. Heart pounding. Right on the lips, too, I can still feel—

But I won't think about it. It's pointless thinking about things like that. I'll think about the letter instead.

✠CHAPTER FIFTEEN✠

"Excuse me, Master, but I seem to have lost Boethius."

He swings around. Glares. Grinds his tooth.

"What?" he splutters.

"I think I must have left Boethius in the kitchen."

Here goes. Please, God, make this work. Please don't let him send someone with me. If he does, I'll have to start all over again.

"In the kitchen?" he growls. "You left that valuable book *in the kitchen?*"

"I don't know. I think so."

He glances around the dormitory. Bernard and Gaubert are collecting stools. Raymond is retrieving the big black psalter from the chest under the window. Amiel has collapsed onto the nearest bed.

He looks very blue today.

"Imbecile!" (*Thwomp!* Clement slams his stick down.) "Brainless fool! Simpleton! How could you lose a book?"

"Master—"

"Go and get it! Right now!"

Yes! Hooray! It worked! Bolting for the door as fast as my legs will carry me.

"Pagan!"

Stop. Turn. He's standing there in the middle of the room: hunched, glowering, ominous.

"Come straight back," he growls, "or I'll come and find you. Is that clear?"

"Yes, Master."

Oh, Pagan, you're so brilliant. Sometimes I'm amazed at how quick you are. Although, to be fair, you shouldn't forget Boethius. Credit where credit's due, Pagan. Who would have thought old Boethius would prove to be such an asset?

Across the herb garden. Turn left. Passing Elias in the corridor: his limp's gone but his eyes are all gummed up. What's wrong with him now? I wonder. Looks bad, whatever it is. Sharp right into the refectory, which still smells of last night's eggs. Bernard Surdellus, sweeping up the dirty rushes.

It's all right, Father, don't look at me like that. I'm here to collect Boethius. Pausing to bow, on my way to the kitchen. Feeling his eyes on my back as I cross the threshold.

Rostand the cook is chopping up carrots.

"Yes?" he mutters, peering through the steam. "What do you want?"

"I left my book."

"Your what?"

"I was here before. With the novices." (Remember? That huddle of pasty mutes, left in one corner to watch the beans soak while Clement was in chapter with the rest of the monks? You must remember. One of them was so excited, he couldn't keep his eyes open.) "I put my book behind that hand screen, so it wouldn't get splashed. But I forgot it."

Pointing at the folded hand screen propped up against the northern wall. Rostand grunts and returns to his vegetables. He looks rather like a peeled vegetable himself: moist, sticky, with raw features that seem to have been hacked out of his face with a blunt kitchen knife. His big hairy paws are covered in flour.

"Go on," he says. "Go and get it. But don't you touch those chestnuts, or I'll skin you alive."

Don't worry. It's not the chestnuts I'm after. Slipping past his sweat-soaked back, kicking my way through the vegetable peelings. Lingering by the fireplace, where something is simmering over a pile of red-hot embers. Soup, is it? Smells like dirty socks.

And there, on the hearthstone—a piece of charcoal, long and straight and perfect. Exactly what I was looking for.

"What's this in here?" (Stooping, as if to sniff at the pungent fumes. Down—down—got it!) "Is it for supper?"

"Leave that stuff alone. That belongs to Father Elias."

"It smells like somebody died."

"*You'll* be dead if you don't get out." Waving his knife at me. "Go on! Hop to it! Before I call Father Clement."

All right, all right, you don't have to shout. Boethius is still lurking where I left him, behind the hand screen. Doesn't seem to have suffered any ill effects. Pick him up, dust him off, head for the door. The outside door. Let's hope that Rostand doesn't ask me where I'm going.

But he's much too busy with his carrots to worry about anything else.

Out into the pale watery light. An overcast day, all damp wind and puddles. Here comes the hard bit. Can I make it to Saurimunda's hole without attracting attention? I can't see anyone, but that doesn't mean I'm not being watched. From the almonry, or the infirmary, or the orchard . . .

Well, it's no good trying to stay hidden. There's nothing to hide behind. I'll just have to pretend I've got Clement's permission to be here. Back straight. Head up. Sauntering along without a care in the world. Who, me? Making trouble? Never. Father Clement told me to go for a little walk. Just to clear my head. I've been studying very hard, you know.

Past the pigsty. Through a strawberry patch. Skirting empty furrows, where the carrots used to be. Somebody's left a basket out in the rain. (There's going to be trouble when Montazin finds out.) The sound of pigs grunting.

Come on, Pagan, nearly there.

Now, where's this hole, exactly? I don't want to spend too much time wandering up and down looking for it. There were bushes, I remember. Spiky bushes. And we went up a slight hill . . .

Over here, perhaps?

This looks promising. Yes! Look here! Footprints in the mud. My footprints, or Saurimunda's? And here's the pile of rubble, all grassy and overgown. This is perfect. If I duck behind this bush, no one will see me from the abbey.

Squatting down, with my back to the wall, opening Boethius. Last page . . . last page . . . here it is. All blank and smooth. Now, where's that charcoal?

Lady Beatrice. (Ugh! How I hate writing with charcoal.) *The coin yo hav been gived is not of yor own. It belong to S Martin. Tak no more coin, or the abbott will heer of yor sinne and the sinne of your cosin Montasin. Be Ware.*

Hmm. I'm not quite sure about some of that spelling. Maybe I should have done it in Latin. But what if she can't read Latin?

What if she can't even read?

Never mind. She's bound to have a chaplain who can read it for her. A chaplain or a notary, or an educated friend. Now, the next problem is tearing this page out. If only it wasn't such tough vellum. (I don't want to smudge the charcoal.) Let's see if I can do it gently. Gently . . . gently . . .

R-r-r-i-ip!

Oh, Lord. I knew that would happen. Most of the *Ware* gone. Still, it could be worse. I'll just squeeze it in again down the bottom. That's it. *Be Ware.* Perfect.

Folding the vellum carefully, so that it doesn't

smudge. Placing it between two stones. Please, God, don't let it rain before Saurimunda comes. Standing up, slowly, with my arms full of Boethius. No one seems to be around . . . oh, yes . . . there's someone. It looks like Roquefire, emerging from the kitchen. Off to feed the pigs. Should I move now, or should I wait? Move, probably. While he's emptying his buckets. Head for the presbytery door: it's always open in the daytime, and there's never anyone in church at this hour. Except for Bernard the White.

Strolling casually across a stretch of grass and gravel. Feeling very exposed. If only I could run! But that would be a mistake. No one runs in a monastery. Running is the surest way of attracting attention. I just have to be calm and relaxed. And humble. Remember you're a monk, Pagan. Remember the twelfth step of humility: "Always let him, with head bent and eyes fixed on the ground, bethink himself of his sins and imagine that he is arraigned before the Dread Judgment of God." Either that, or the Dread Judgment of Father Clement. If Clement ever finds out what I've done to the back of this book, he'll slice me into very small pieces and nail every piece to this dormitory wall.

Over the threshold; into the church. Nearly

there now. Shuffling past the sacristy, the Abbot's chair, the altar. (Stop; bow; genuflect.) Turn left, and through the cloister door. Gerard's working at the book presses: he gives me a suspicious glance. Go boil your bladder, Gerard. A low buzz of voices from the gathering of monks by the latrines. What's happened now? Something pretty exciting, by the look of it. Maybe Sicard's got rid of that wart at long last. Or perhaps Bernard Magnus is constipated. I can't wait to find out.

Plunging into the dimness of the corridor and—

Bang!

Straight into Clement.

"Where have you been?" he snarls.

"I went to the kitchen—"

"I was just in the kitchen, and you weren't there!"

"No, Master. Neither was Boethius. I must have left the book in church, after our last office."

Nice footwork, Pagan. Very nimble. He squints at me in a threatening way, and his knuckles turn white as he squeezes the top of his stick.

"Are you lying to me, Pagan?"

"No, Master."

"Because if you are, you'll suffer for it. Remember what I told you about lying. I told you that lying is an abomination to the Lord."

Yes, you did tell me that. But you also told me that it's a readily believable argument. Which tends to be the way I look at it myself.

"Yes, Master."

"And the Lord is terrible in his punishments, Pagan."

"Yes, Master."

"So will you tell the truth and repent, or lie and suffer the Lord's punishment?"

It's no good, Clement. You'll have to do better than that. Meeting his gaze and returning it, unflinchingly. Chin up. Wide-eyed. Ingenuous.

"Master, I have been telling the truth."

Whoops! Is he going to hit me? No, I'm safe. He turns on his heel and shuffles back down the corridor.

"Come on!" he barks. "Get moving! We've wasted enough time already through your carelessness!"

Not what you'd call a graceful loser.

As for me, I suppose I'll just have to wait. Wait and watch, and pray that it keeps fine until tomorrow morning.

Because I'm certainly not doing this again.

✝CHAPTER SIXTEEN✝

"Roquefire! Roquefire!"

Who—? What—? What's going on? What's all the noise? Thumping and screaming . . .

"Roquefire, come back! Don't leave me!"

That sounds like Saurimunda. I don't understand. Is it a nightmare? Am I still asleep? Turning over, sitting up. It *is* Saurimunda! Clearly visible in the soft glow of the nightlight, sobbing and screaming and banging at the door.

God preserve us.

"Silence!" It's Clement. He's on his feet, and so is Roland. They're both hovering, unsure of what to do. Clement waves his stick at her. "Silence! I command you to be silent!"

Suddenly the door bursts open. Saurimunda is pushed back, and hits the ground with a thud as Montazin appears on the threshold.

He's fully dressed, with a lamp in his hand. Tall. Majestic. Forbidding. Don't tell me he's on circator duty.

"What's going on?" he cries. "Who is this woman?"

No response. Saurimunda's whimpering, her face shiny and wet. This is insane. What's happening here? Why couldn't she get the door open? Was someone holding it from the outside? I don't understand. . . .

"Who admitted this woman?" Montazin takes a step forward. He points at Roland. "You? Did you admit her?"

Roland shakes his head.

"What about you?" This time Montazin points at Gaubert, who nearly hits the roof.

"Me?" he squeaks. (It's almost laughable.)

Saurimunda makes a dash for the door, but Montazin is too quick for her.

"Oh, no, you don't." He grabs her wrist and pulls it so hard that she yelps. She also drops something. Montazin picks it up.

It's a leather pouch.

"I didn't steal it!" she moans. "Roquefire gave it to me —"

Thwack! He chops her across the face. All right, that's it. I've had enough of you, you bastard.

"Stop that! Keep your hands to yourself!"

Everyone turns and stares. Uh-oh. Now I'm really in trouble.

Clement makes signs at me. *Where—your— pouch?* Trust him to follow the Rule. Even in this moment of crisis, he remembers that we're not supposed to be talking. He flaps a hand at Bernard, who struggles with the chest under my bed. Drags it out. Throws open the lid. Rummages among the spare socks and shirts.

No pouch, of course. Doesn't surprise me. This whole thing is beginning to smell like a setup.

"I swear, Master, I haven't touched my pouch since last Tues—"

Clement strikes the floor with his stick. He puts his finger to his lips and draws it up and down. *Silence!*

Montazin tosses the pouch onto my bed.

Oh, yes, it's mine, all right. Somebody must have got in here and stolen it when I wasn't around. Montazin? Roquefire? Those scumbags. Those festering maggots. Clement reaches over and picks it up. Examines it. Drops it. And suddenly stiffens, like a hunting dog on a stag's scent.

There's something else tangled in the covers: something bright and pretty.

A red petticoat.

Hold on—this is insane. It's unbelievable. "Master, it's a trick! Can't you see what's happening? Someone's playing a trick on me!"

Clement jerks his finger again. *Silence!* Oh, no. Not yet, old man. Not until I've had my say.

"No! I won't be silent! Do you really think I'd be stupid enough to bring a woman in here? Into this dormitory? Into this bed? You must be out of your minds!" Peeling Clement's hand off my mouth, as he tries to gag me. "This is Roquefire's doing! He must have brought her in! Ask her! Ask her who brought her here! It was Roquefire, wasn't it?"

"Yes." A shrill, frightened squeak. She's seen me now. There's hope on her face. "It was Roquefire. He said he wanted to show me something. Then he pushed me in here and shut the door—"

Thwack! Another of Montazin's blows, this time across her ear. You bastard. You evil bastard. I'm going to kill you, Montazin.

"Naturally this wicked novice would blame Roquefire," he spits. "Just to save his own skin. He is a liar, as well as a fornicator."

"But didn't you hear what she said?" Appealing

156

to Clement, whose expression is a mixture of doubt and disgust. Please, Clement, please, where's your intelligence? "She just *said* it was Roquefire! She said so herself!"

"She? *She?* Are we to believe this harlot?" Montazin sneers as Saurimunda writhes in his grasp. "If it was Roquefire's doing, then where is he? I didn't see anyone."

"That's because you sent him!" Slapping Clement's hand away again. "That's because you planned all this! Do you think I don't know? Do you think I'm a fool? You panicked, because of that letter I wrote—"

"Silence!" Montazin's losing his self-control. The veins stand out like ropes in his neck. "Insolent Turk! How dare you speak to me like that?"

"Master, please . . ." (Listen, Clement, I'm begging you.) "Why do you think she couldn't get the door open? Because someone was holding it shut from outside! This is all a trick, to get me expelled. Because I know things about the cellarer—"

"*Yeowch!*"

It's Montazin's voice; Saurimunda's teeth are buried in his hand. He drops her wrist, and she bolts like a hare.

"Ow—ah—ouch . . ."

157

Bernard snickers. Saurimunda disappears. Montazin doubles up, groaning, his wound tucked under his armpit.

There's a brief, stunned silence.

"Leave her," the cellarer finally remarks. "Let her go. She's just a dirty little slut of a peasant." He straightens up and tries to shake the pain from his hand. "She's not the real sinner," he gasps. "The real sinner is still in this room."

"Yes, you're right! And it's you, you hypocrite!" Turning to Clement. Gripping his arm. "Please—Master—you've got to listen to me—"

Oof! Reeling back, as he pushes me away.

"Silence!" he hisses. "If you say one more word—*one more word*—I'm going to throw you out of this monastery! *Do you understand?*"

"Master." It's Roland. Very pale, very agitated. He steps forward. "Master, I know this can't be Pagan's doing—"

"Silence!" Clement stamps his foot. "There *must* be silence!" He puts his right hand under his cheek, and closes his eyes. (*Sleep.*) He holds his clasped hands out in front of him. (*We.*) He makes a flapping duck's bill. (*Talk.*) He draws a circle in the air. (*Tomorrow.*)

Sleep. We—talk—tomorrow.

And all at once, the bells start ringing. God preserve us. It is tomorrow.

As Clement claps his hands, there's a sudden rush for belts and scapulars. Raymond fumbles with his blanket, drawing it up over his pillow. Gaubert begins to pull on his boots. Roland stands there, helpless.

Montazin reels off a rapid series of signs, aimed directly at Clement. *I—go—infirmary. We—talk—chapter.*

Clement nods, and Montazin disappears. I hope he breaks his neck on the infirmary staircase. I hope his bite swells up, and he dies of blood poisoning. I hope he goes straight to hell and spends eternity roasting on a slow spit over a blazing fire.

Jesus Christ our Lord, what am I going to do? It's beginning to sink in, at last. The awful realization.

You've done it now, Pagan. You've really done it now. Who's going to believe a word you say? You don't have any proof. It's your word against the cellarer's, and he's been here since God created Adam.

O Lord my God, deliver me from mine enemies. Defend me from them that rise up against me. Deliver me from the workers of iniquity and save me from the bloody men.

For lo, they lie in wait for my soul: the mighty are gathered against me.

CHAPTER SEVENTEEN

Thwoomp!

Oh, God. Don't cry, Pagan. You're not going to cry, not in front of Montazin.

Thwoomp!

Don't think about the pain. Think about something else. Think about . . . think about revenge. That's it. Think about skewering Montazin's eyeballs, and serving them up lightly boiled with a mushroom salad.

Thwoomp!

How many more? Six? Seven? I've lost count. And every blow is worse than the one before.

I think Montazin is trying to kill me.

Thwoomp!

Wish I was standing up. Why are they making me lie face-down on the floor? Because they're scared of looking me straight in the eye?

Thwoomp!

God, God, God, this is—this is tough. This is really tough.

Please, God, make this finish soon.

"Reverend Father!"

Who's that? Is it Roland? His voice sounds strange.

"Reverend Father—please—you mustn't do this." A hoarse, gasping voice. "This is wrong, very wrong—"

"Sit down, Roland." (Guilabert.) "You are not permitted to speak in chapter."

"But—"

"Sit down!"

Poor Roland. Don't fret, my lord, I've had worse than this. When I was at Saint Joseph's, they practically flogged the skin off my back every second week.

Thwoomp!

Oh. Ah. But I have to admit, I'd forgotten what it felt like.

Sudden noise. Sounds like . . . footsteps? Turn my head, and it's Roland. Can't see much above his ankles, but I recognize the way he moves. Rushing past me, out the door. Leaving a shocked silence that Guilabert finally breaks.

"Continue," he says.

Thwoomp!

It can't last much longer. If it does, he'll have all the skin off my back. I know it. I can feel it. Surely they don't want blood all over their chapter-house floor?

Thwoomp!

Make haste, O God, to deliver me; make haste to help me, O Lord. Let them be ashamed and confounded that seek after my soul: let them be turned backward, and put to confusion, that desire my hurt—

Thwoomp!

God damn you to hell, Montazin, you devil's spawn, you whore of Babylon, I'm going to get you, and I'm going to break you, and you're going to wish you were dead and buried.

Thwoomp!

"Enough," says Guilabert. (Oh, God. Thank you, God.)

"Get up, Pagan."

I don't even know if I can get up. Slowly, stiffly, pushing myself onto my knees. Can I take my hands off the floor? Everything's shaking like a tree in a gale. First foot. Second foot. Rising like Lazarus.

Jesus, but my back hurts. I can hardly breathe, it hurts so much.

"Put your clothes on, Pagan." Guilabert, sitting right in front of me. Close enough to spit at. Pale and flaccid, like a great, quivering heap of poached egg whites. "Brother Montazin, help him with the back of that robe, will you?"

Montazin. Standing there, breathless, with the stick dangling from his long, elegant fingers. He drops the stick, and reaches for me. Oh, no, you don't, you unspeakable vermin. If you touch me again—if you lay one more finger on me—I'll kill you. I swear it. I'll flay you alive.

Knocking his hand away. Dragging my shirt back over my shoulders. Tugging at the strings of my robe. Ow! Ouch! God, how the scapular burns.

"Pagan Kidrouk." Guilabert intones it like a psalm. "You have been chastised for a terrible sin, the sin of fornication, which is forbidden by the Holy Rule and by Saint Paul the Apostle, who wrote: 'He that committeth fornication sinneth against his own body.' Do you repent of this sin, and ask forgiveness of your brothers in Christ?"

My brothers in Christ. That's a good one. What brothers are we talking about? Montazin, perhaps? I can't see Montazin anymore (he's standing behind me), but I know what must be written on his face. I can't see Raymond, either, but I'm sure he's enjoying the show. As for Clement, I'm surprised he didn't wade in and finish the flogging himself.

"Pagan? Answer me. Do you repent of your sin?"

"I didn't commit any sin."

A murmur from around the room. Guilabert sighs impatiently.

"Do you still persist in denying that you committed fornication?" he says.

"I didn't commit anything! It was all a trick! The cellarer—"

"Silence!" Guilabert purses his lips and makes a sour face, as if he's been licking lemons. "This assembly will not soil its ears with your wicked and deceitful tales. You are a sinful creature, Pagan Kidrouk. You are sick with the sickness of impudence and hypocrisy."

He takes a deep breath, and continues in such heavy, baleful accents that you'd think he was announcing the end of the world.

"In cases such as yours, Pagan, the Holy Rule rec-

164

ommends first applying the ointments of exhortation. If that should fail, as it has with you, then the medicine of the Holy Scriptures should be administered. Next comes the final cautery of scourging. If this has no effect, the Rule advises prayer, that the Lord (who can do all things) may work the cure of the sick brother. Finally, the Rule says: 'If he is not healed by this means, then let the Abbot use the severing knife according to the saying of the Apostle, "Put away the evil one from among you, lest one diseased sheep should infect the whole flock.' This is what the Rule advises us, Pagan."

A long pause. Does that mean what I think it means? If only the Abbot were here! Guilabert leans forward and puts his pudgy hands together.

"If you do not repent," he concludes, "then you will be expelled from this monastery."

So there it is: the final threat. Stand firm and go, or submit and stay. I knew it was coming. The question is, what should I do?

But there's only one answer. Of course I'm staying. I've got some unfinished business to complete.

"Reverend Father." Trying to bow. God, my back! "Reverend Father, I humbly beseech you to pardon my sins, that I may rejoin this holy brotherhood."

Tears pricking my eyes. Tears of anger, not shame.

I'm not ashamed. Why should I be? I've licked dirt-ier boots than his.

Get a grip on yourself, Pagan. Never let anyone see you cry.

"You are forgiven, but not absolved," says Guilabert. He shifts around, grimacing. (Perhaps his left buttock has gone to sleep.) "You will pro-ceed from this place to the church, and pray there until Sext," he continues. "During the services, you will prostrate yourself before the altar, and you will remain there, during every office, until every monk has left the church. You will do this until I and the novice-master believe that you are truly repen-tant." He lifts his gaze and fixes it on someone behind me. "You novices: You have been invited to chapter this day to witness the punishment of an unrepentant sinner. Let his sufferings be an example to you. Now go to the kitchen and reflect on what you have just seen. You can go too, Pagan."

With pleasure. If I have to look at your fat face anymore, I'm going to be sick. Casting one quick glance around, just to find Montazin. He's stand-ing there with his hands in his sleeves. Smiling a little. He sees me looking and narrows his eyes.

You wait, Montazin. Just you wait. You're dead meat on a stick, pus-bag.

It's hard to walk. My robe feels like molten chain mail, rubbing against my shoulders. But I'll make it somehow, even if it kills me. Out of the chapter house. Crippling into the cloister. Turn right, and past the book presses. It's still raining.

The church is cold and dark.

My stumbling footsteps, echoing across the tiles. Huge stone pillars marching off into the shadows. A black shape crouched in front of the altar.

Roland.

He's on his knees, with his face in his hands. Praying? Crying? Please don't let him be crying. I'll never be able to make it if he is.

"My lord?"

He looks up. No tears, but such misery — such sickly gray shock, and despair —

"Oh, my lord, it's all right. It wasn't too bad."

He shuts his eyes and groans.

"Please, my lord, I've had worse. Much worse. I used to get beaten all the time. You must have seen the scars. . . ."

He buries his face in his hands again. Mumbles something through his fingers. It's too quick to catch.

"Pardon? I didn't quite —"

"We're leaving." Hoarsely. "We'll leave as soon as you want."

Leave? Are you serious? Squatting down, so I'm level with his right ear. "But why should we leave, my lord? I've made my submission. They're not going to expel me now."

He turns his head. Up close, you can see the little wrinkles forming on his brow and in the corners of his eyes. His nose seems to go on forever. "You made your submission?" he says. "But you told me it was all a trick. . . ."

"Well, of course it was!"

"Then why—"

"Because I don't want to get expelled! Not now. That's just what the cellarer was planning." Oh, yes. Because I've hit a nerve with him. That letter was right on target. Montazin is channeling alms to Beatrice de Mazeroles, and Aeldred is acting as his courier. I'm sure of it. "What I've got to do now is hang on until I can find some proof. Some fragment of proof. Otherwise the Abbot won't believe me. Not after last night. Everyone's going to think I'm a lying little fornicator."

"Pagan—"

"But Montazin's going to pay for this. I'm telling you. He's going to pay for every stripe on my back."

"Oh, Pagan." He's wringing his hands. "Oh, Pagan, I don't know what to do. What am I going to do?"

"My lord—"

"Don't call me that! I'm not a lord! I can't protect you—I have no authority—I've forsworn my arms, but I can't—I can't stand there and let them—"

"Roland. Calm down."

"It's so hard," he whispers. "Why is it all so hard?"

Don't ask me. I'm just an illegitimate Arab with a very sore back.

He sighs and presses both hands to his temples. "I can't bear it," he says. "I just can't bear it anymore."

Bear what? What are you talking about? You're not talking about me, are you?

"My lord—I mean, Roland—do you remember what you told me last summer? When we joined?"

He looks perplexed. "Last summer?" he echoes.

"You said it was hurting you to see me jumping to your defense. You said I should forget about you, and look to my own path. Do you remember that?"

"Of course." He nods. "Of course I do."

"Well then, don't you understand that it works both ways? Don't you realize how much it hurts me to see you upset like this? It doesn't make me feel any better, you know."

A pause, as he thinks. I wish I knew what was

169

wrong with him. He's never been a particularly happy person, but ever since Esclaramonde . . . I don't know. It's as if something's broken.

Perhaps he's still grieving. Perhaps he'll get over it, eventually. Or perhaps it has something to do with his change of occupation; after spending all his life as a knight, riding around in the open air, it must be difficult to adapt to a monastery. Perhaps he's not coping with the fasts and the lack of exercise.

"You're right," he says in a dull voice. "I have my own path. I must look to my own path."

"And you mustn't worry about me. I know what I'm doing." (Ouch! God! My back!) He hears me grunt, and winces.

"You should go to the infirmary," he says.

"I can't. I have to stay here and pray."

"But your back—"

"It's all right. Really. I'll manage."

I will manage, too. I'll get through tonight without shedding a tear. I'll keep my head low, and my mouth shut. I'll stick on Montazin's trail like a lymer hound.

And when I find the proof I need, I'll see him flogged until he can't stand up straight.

WINTER 1188–1189

❖

‡ CHAPTER EIGHTEEN ‡

It's Jerusalem. It's got to be. A narrow street, lined with shops; the sun beating down on colored awnings. And isn't that Saurimunda? Hovering in a doorway, beckoning, smiling. . . . But it's hard to see, because she's wearing a veil. A veil and a gauzy . . . wait. It isn't her at all. It's someone much older. Someone tall and dark, with big breasts—*huge* breasts—heavy and smooth—

Dong. Dong. Dong.

Oh, no! Please don't run away! Come back! It's nothing! It's just a church bell . . .

Dong. Dong. Dong.

On second thought, it's not a church bell. It's a hand bell. This is crazy. This doesn't make sense. Where did the shops go? Something banging—

Hold on, what's under my head? Feels like wool. Darkness. Footsteps. Oh, God. Now I understand.

It's time to wake up.

Bernard Blancus, ringing his bell on the threshold. *Dong. Dong. Dong.* I don't believe this: surely it can't be nocturnes? I only just closed my eyes! Amiel, in the next bed, throwing back his covers. I can't do that; it's freezing in here! Burying my face in the pillow. Please, please, let me go back to my dream. Let me go back to the big-breasted lady.

A sudden shaft of cold air, as Clement pulls my covers back. He raps at my bed with his stick.

All right, all right, I'm coming.

Feet first. Ow! Ah! This floor is like ice! Where are my socks? Quick, my socks! Fumbling around for my belt, my socks, my scapular. My wonderful winter cape. My sheepskin gloves—

A tap on the shoulder.

It's Clement. He makes the sign for "where," and runs one finger down the middle of his face (a reference to Roland's aristocratic nose).

Where—Roland?

What do you mean, where's Roland? Looking around. It's hard to see, in this light: a bunch of shadowy figures, milling around, making beds, pulling on

174

clothes, yawning, coughing, spitting. But none of them is big enough or broad enough to be Roland.

God preserve us. Where is he?

Making a fist, with the thumb turned down. *I know not.* Clement frowns and peers at me closely. What are you looking at me like that for? I just told you, I don't know where he is! Maybe he's gone to the latrines! Maybe he's sick!

Oh, Lord. I hope not. I hope he's not sick. Signing at Clement: *I—go—infirmary.* Clement shakes his head.

You—go—church, he replies, and heads for the door.

Damn it, Roland, where are you? Why didn't you wake me up? Fumbling with my boots as the others follow Clement, trailing after him like a flock of little black chicks. Hurry, Pagan, hurry! Don't want to be late. One boot on. Other boot on. Joining the end of the line, just as it enters the herb garden. Past the refectory. Stumbling along in the dimness.

I knew this would happen. Roland's been so odd lately. So quiet. And not eating nearly enough. Getting much too thin. But of course he won't say anything, not even when we have a chance to talk—which is practically never. Oh, Roland, Roland, where are you?

Emerging from the corridor, into a steady flow of monks. Heads down, cowls up, all making for the church's southern entrance. Dense, black, face-less shadows. Not a sound except for the shuffling of feet and the chorus of bubbling winter coughs, as we cross the threshold into the nave. Icy drafts whistling around our ankles. Gold leaf glittering in the candlelight. The sweet, painted face of the Holy Virgin, with the Christ child in her arms. And there—over there! That's Roland! He moves away from the altar, stiffly, as if his knees are hurt-ing him. Don't tell me he's been *praying* in here! What's the point of praying at night, when we have to do it all day? If I linger at the end of the line, he'll be able to catch up with me. What's the matter, Roland? You look like a wreck. Your face is all bones and dark smudges.

Clement signs at him. *You—absent.* Roland puts his gloved hands together, signifying "prayer." It seems to satisfy Clement. He nods and moves into his place. Roland nudges me forward. No, Roland, you can go first. I want to stay as far away from Clement as possible. The farther away I am, the better my chances are of getting you to tell me what's wrong.

"*Domine labia mea aperies, et os meum annuntiabit laudem tuam.*"

The chanting begins. It's a little raw and ragged: I don't think everyone's really awake yet. I know I'm not. Roland clears his throat and tries to follow the verses. Even after all this time, he's still not very confident.

"*Domine, quam multi sunt qui tribulant . . .*"

Roland. Roland! Tugging at his sleeve. He looks down, blinking.

I have to mouth the words, because I don't know what the signs are. *What's wrong?* (Emphasizing each word.) *What's the matter?*

He shakes his head and turns away. In God's name, Roland, what's that supposed to mean?

"*Penes Dominum est salus super populum tuum sit benedictio tua . . .*"

Roland! Look at me, damn you! Pulling at his robe again. This time he doesn't even glance down; he just takes my hand and gently pushes it aside.

"*Venite, exsultemus Domino, iubilemus Deo . . .*"

All right, if that's the way you want it. Reaching up. Finding his arm. Giving it a sharp pinch.

He jumps like a rabbit. Clement turns and scowls down the row at us. I didn't do a thing! Honestly! I was just chanting the "Gloria." Look, I've got my hands in my sleeves and everything. How could I have pinched him?

Slowly, reluctantly, Clement looks away.

And Roland still won't even cast a glance in my direction. Very well. Don't, then. See if I care. You're impossible, Roland, you never tell me anything. You just bottle it up inside—let it tear you to pieces—and you won't even let me help! I know I said we had our own paths to follow, but I didn't mean that they should be completely walled in.

"De profundis clamavi, ad te, Domine; Domine, exaudi vocem meam . . ."

Psalm One Hundred and—what? Twenty-nine? Thirty? A slow, sad rhythm, deep and hollow, swelling to a full chorus at the end of the first verse. "Out of the depths I cried unto Thee, O Lord; O Lord, hear my voice." The piercing, pleading cry of the oblates, high and sweet, rising to the vaults—catching on the highest note—and suddenly falling again, in gentle steps, weary and wistful. "Let Thine ears be attentive to my supplication." A quiet passage, now, throbbing like a heartbeat. Asking for forgiveness. How sad it is.

How unbearably sad. Why do we have to sing this at nocturnes? I'm miserable enough as it is, so early in the morning.

"*Sustinuit anima mea in verbum eius; speravit anima mea in Domino.*"

Beside me, Roland coughs. It's just a spasm, muffled in his chest. A slight shudder. His voice fails halfway through the sixth verse: "My soul waiteth for the Lord, more than they that watch for the morning." What an appropriate image. The morning is exactly what I'm watching for, because a little sunlight may serve to thaw my frozen feet.

More shudders from Roland. I hope it's not a choking fit. Glancing up at his face . . .

And it's wet.

It's wet. He's crying. His whole body shakes with suppressed sobs.

Sweet saints preserve us.

"*Quia apud Dominum misericordia et copiosa apud eum redemptio . . .*"

Roland. Roland! Grabbing his arm. He turns his face away and wipes his eyes. But his chest is still heaving. Oh, God, oh, God, what is it? What's wrong? In God's name, Roland, don't shut me out! I can't bear it!

"*Et ipse redimet Israel ex omnibus iniquitatibus eius.*"

179

The last, lingering verse, hanging in the air like a silver thread—a thin, pure, extended sound. Roland sniffs: he takes a deep breath, and another, and another. (Seems to be calming down.) With an immense effort, he brings himself under control again.

But he's not going to tell me what's wrong. I just know he isn't. He's going to let it eat away at his heart until it breaks, and then I'll be left to pick up the pieces.

O Lord, I beg you, won't you ease his burden? Whatever it is, he doesn't deserve to suffer like this. He's a good man. He's doing his best. Please, God, please, take away his sorrow. Lift up his soul and enlighten his darkness.

You're the only one who can help him, because he won't take any help from me.

CHAPTER NINETEEN

"What's this?" Rainier pretends to be very, very puzzled. "What are you doing back on this stool, little man? Haven't you already been shaved?"

Ha, ha. Pardon me while I sew up my sides. "No, I haven't, Father." (But I *have* heard all your bumfluff jokes before, so why don't you give them a rest?) "My mustache has been growing, see?"

"Bless you, boy, that's not a mustache! That's a smudge of charcoal!" He beams around at his snickering audience: a gaggle of monks all lined up along the cloister walls like crows along a fence. "What you need for that mustache is a bit of damp cloth," he continues. "You don't need a razor!"

Well, maybe not, pus-bag, but *you* certainly do. If someone doesn't take a scythe to those eyebrows pretty soon, you won't be able to see out from under them. What kind of fertilizer do you use on them, anyway? Manure or rotten vegetable peelings?

"All right, Father." (You big fat swill-pot.) "If you don't want to shave my jaw, perhaps you can do my head. There's no lack of growth up there." In contrast to the windswept desert on your own scalp, Baldy. But I'd better not say it aloud—not while he's carrying a razor.

Honestly. I ask you. Why do I have to put up with this? Every single shaving day, it's the same old thing. Other people don't have to put up with this. Why am I always the one?

"Very well, Midge, I'll clean up your tonsure for you." He winks as he wipes his razor on the skirts of his robe. "And I'll keep the clippings, so you can make up a proper mustache for next time. With flour paste."

More mindless giggles. Everyone's laughing except Roland and Clement: Clement because he doesn't know how to, Roland because he's lost in thought. Moping around, as usual. I really have to talk to Roland; I have to find out what's wrong.

And there's no point waiting for a private moment, either, because private moments don't exist anymore. I'll just have to do it when I'm finished here, and damn the eavesdroppers.

Brrr! Gasping as Rainier slaps on the water. One day, when I'm an old, old monk, I might be first in line and get shaved with *hot* water, instead of the tepid dregs we novices always end up with. Cold shaves, cold food, cold feet; the essence of winter at Saint Martin's.

A blast of wind turns my head to ice.

"Sit still, boy, or I'll have your ear off." Rainier, scraping away up there. A fitful buzz of conversation. The drip, drip, drip of water off the eaves, as they shed the residue of last night's rainstorm.

What a dreary, damp, uninspiring day.

"There you go." A slap on the neck from Rainier. "Just one more rinse—that's it—and you're all tidied up. Who's next? Gaubert? Come on, Pagan, get a move on."

I'm moving, I'm moving. Off the stool, across to Roland. Squeezing in next to him. Nudging his elbow. He looks up and blinks.

"Pagan . . ." he murmurs. His cheeks are all raw where Rainier's been at them.

"You're cut, my lord."

"What?"

"You've got a cut. On your cheek." (And were lucky to escape with your head, knowing Rainier.) "Shall I get some cobwebs?"

"No, no, don't trouble yourself." He blinks again and rubs his eyes, almost as if he's been sleeping. "You mustn't call me that, Pagan. I've told you not to call me that."

"Call you what?"

"I'm not your lord anymore. I'm your brother."

"Oh, really?" Lowering my voice. "Then why don't you treat me like a brother? Why don't you tell me what's wrong, instead of sulking away like a two-year-old?"

"Pagan—"

"I'm not stupid, you know. I'm not blind." (Softly now, Pagan, or you'll have Clement listening in.) "It's quite obvious that you're miserable. It's written all over your face. But how can you expect anyone to help if you don't talk about it?"

"I have talked about it."

Pause.

What?

He's looking down at his boots.

"What do you mean?" In God's name, Roland! "What do you mean, you've talked about it?"

"In confession."

In *confession?* You mean you—you mean you've talked to someone else? And not to me? You've gone to someone else about this?

God, I can hardly . . . this is . . . I'm having trouble breathing . . .

"You went to someone *else?*"

"Pagan—"

"Oh, well, if you went to someone else, that's all right, then! Since they've obviously done you so much good! I mean, I can see that they've really put your mind at rest, there! Really cheered you up!"

"Will you stop being so childish?"

"No, Roland, *you* stop being so childish! Do you think you're the only one with troubles? You don't even know . . . I can't even . . . If you had any idea!"

Suddenly aware of the silence. Looking around, and everyone's staring. Staring at me. What happened? What's wrong? What am I doing on my feet, like this?

Quickly sitting down again.

"If something's troubling you, Pagan," Clement says at last, "there are people you can see. In private. Carrying on like a mad hen isn't going to solve your problems."

185

God preserve us.

"Unless, perhaps, you'd like to share your troubles with the whole abbey?" He's lifting his lip in a sneer. "Is that what you want to do?"

"No, Master."

"No. Good. Then kindly don't raise your voice again."

I think I'm going to die of embarrassment. Quick—hurry—somebody say something! Clement turns back to Elias and continues his interrupted lecture on the merits of garlic oil. Rainier invites his next victim to sit down. Gerard farts and apologizes.

Roland won't even look at me.

"Aha! There he is!" Bernard Incentor sits up straight. He waves frantically at the figure emerging from the guesthouse entrance. "Raymond! Here! Over here! I've saved a seat for you."

God, and now Raymond's back. Just what I needed. He strolls across the cloister garth, looking smug and self-satisfied; he's carrying several small pots and a little leather bag.

"It's honey," he says as he stops in front of Clement. "Honey for the novices, and a donation for the abbey. With my father's compliments."

"How very kind of your father." Clement doesn't

sound too impressed, but then he never sounds impressed about anything. "You must give it to Brother Montazin. He'll take care of it. Give it to him now."

Brother Montazin. Sitting on the next bench with Guilabert and Sicard and all the other really *important* monks. Deep in conversation about really important things. Self-important expression on his razor-nicked face.

Accepting the gifts wordlessly.

I wonder if that little bag of money will end up in Lady Beatrice's pocket. Bound to, I should think. Look at the way Montazin just slips it under his scapular (out of sight, out of mind) as he mutters into Guilabert's ear. Oh, you're a sly one, aren't you? Butter wouldn't melt, you scorpion. But I know you. I'm watching you. One slip, pus-bag, and you've had it, my friend.

"How's your father?" Bernard asks the question before Raymond has even reached our bench. "How are Lady Saurina and Lady Constance?"

"They're in good health," Raymond replies. He's so very, very pleased with himself, so very pleased to be the only novice ever to receive visits from his family. Describing how his eldest brother has bought a new horse, and how his youngest sister is

187

going to get married next month, while all the poor, abandoned novices cluster around eagerly, drinking in every word. All the abandoned novices bar one, that is. *I'm* not interested in Raymond's boring family news. I've got other things to think about.

"Are there any other guests in there?" (Durand, hovering at Raymond's elbow.) "Anyone interesting?"

"Oh, there's the almoner's cousin. That foreigner. You know, the one who always comes." Raymond glances at Clement—who's still discussing garlic oil—and continues in hushed tones: "Actually, he was in the room next to my father's. And he was having an argument. You could hear it right through the wall."

An argument? "With whom?" It's out before I can stop it.

Raymond turns to glare at me, a haughty expression on his stuck-up face.

"I wasn't talking to you," he says.

"But was it the almoner? Was he arguing with the almoner?"

"Maybe." Which means yes, of course; I can tell by the fleeting look of annoyance that rumples His

Majesty's forehead. Durand presses for more information.

"What did they say, Raymond? What did they say? Go on, tell us—"

"Hush! Don't shout! Do you want everyone to hear?" Raymond's voice drops to a conspiratorial whisper: he puts one hand on Bernard's shoulder, and the other on Durand's, and pulls them both toward him. "They were arguing about money," he says, "if you really want to know. They were arguing because the almoner owed his cousin some money."

"Why?"

"If I knew, Bernard, I'd tell you. But I wasn't going to sit there with my ear to the door. That's the sort of thing a servant would do." Raymond throws a sideways look at me from out of his long gray eyes. "Only scum eavesdrop," he adds, meaning, of course, that I should move out of his immediate neighborhood.

But Durand seems puzzled.

"I don't understand," he says. "Our monks don't have any money, not for themselves. So how could they owe any?"

"Well, I'm just telling you what I heard, Durand.

Maybe I've got it wrong. But I do know they didn't seem to like each other very much." Raymond yawns, displaying a fine set of teeth. "The way they were carrying on!" he exclaims. "It was really rough. In fact, I'm surprised the cousin even bothers to visit."

Well, I'm not. I'm not at all surprised. This simply must have something to do with that Lady Beatrice business; the question is, what? What's the connection? And why would Aeldred be paying money to a cousin he can't stand? Unless . . . wait a moment . . .

"Raymond?"

"What?" It's almost funny, the level of revulsion he manages to convey in a single word. "What do you want now?"

"I was wondering if you could tell me, confidentially of course . . ." (Keep it down, Pagan. Don't let Montazin hear.) "I was wondering if you could tell me how long the almoner's cousin has been showing up?"

"Why?"

Dear, oh, dear, it's like squeezing water from a stone. "Well, I was only wondering, but if you can't tell me—"

"Of course I can tell you!" (Ha. I knew he'd jump

at that bait. So proud of being informed.) "The almoner's cousin has been visiting every month, for six months," he says. "But why would you want to know that?"

"Just interested." Very interested. So it's been six months, has it? Exactly the length of time that Aeldred's been visiting his lady friend.

I think I'm onto something, here.

"Novices!" Clement's voice cuts through the air like a Turkish mace. "Brother Rainier's finished with you now, so we're going back to the dormitory. All rise, please."

Curse it, not the dormitory! I need to visit that guesthouse. I need to talk to that cousin. Unless Aeldred's still there . . . but he's not. He's back here, with Montazin. Must have joined us after Raymond did.

Come on, Pagan, concentrate. What are you going to do?

"This way, novices." Clement heads for the herb garden, disappearing into the long, icy tunnel that links the garden to the cloisters. It's dark in there. Do you think if I . . . ? But I'd have to be quick . . .

Waiting as Roland follows Clement: first Roland, and Raymond next, and Durand, and Gaubert, all in a straight line, with Bernard and Ademar bringing

191

up the rear. Dawdling after them, carefully, so that I'm still in the shadowy passage by the time they've turned the corner.

Now! Quick! Fingers down the throat, and let's get started. Think snot pies. Think roast turds. Think vomit . . .

Gagging. Choking.

"Pagan?" Bernard's voice, from somewhere nearby. "Master! Come quickly! Pagan's throwing up!"

A valuable skill I first learned many years ago, at Saint Joseph's. Still comes in handy. Oooh. Auugh. The sound of Clement's walking stick: *rap-rap, rap-rap.*

"Pagan?" His feet are hovering at the edge of my mess. "What's wrong?"

Groaning.

"It must be something he ate," Gaubert squeaks. "I felt sick myself, last night—"

"Silence! Go back to the dormitory. You too, Roland. All of you." With my face against the wall like this, it's impossible to see them go, but their shuffling footsteps fade away like the colors of sunset. Only Clement remains.

"Come on, Pagan." He touches my arm. "I'll take you to the infirmary."

Groan.

"Yes, yes, I know you don't feel well. But we'll get you to bed, and you'll soon feel better. Come on now, it's not very far."

God preserve us, he sounds almost human. Could it really be pity? Or is it some kind of trick?

He totters like a newborn calf when I lean on him.

"That's it. Just a few steps," he says. "And then Brother Elias will put you to bed, and he'll give you a draft, and in no time at all you'll be well enough to come back and clean up this disgusting mess you've made. Incidentally," he adds as we lurch through the almonry door, "if you've been eating stolen food, Pagan, you must expect this kind of punishment. 'Evil pursueth sinners, but to the righteous good shall be repayed.'"

God preserve us. Doesn't he *ever* let up?

CHAPTER TWENTY

"Ugh! Yuck!"

"Drink it, Pagan."

"But it tastes like—"

"I know it tastes horrible. All medicines taste horrible. Now drink it."

God preserve us. Tastes like the floor of a leper's latrine. "What is this stuff, anyway, goats' piss?"

"It's lovage and anise seed and—well—other things. It's to settle your stomach." Elias lifts his head as the sound of bells penetrates the walls of the infirmary. "That's the bell for Sext," he remarks. "It's Mass, so I'll have to go. Can you and Amiel look after each other while I'm away? I won't be long."

"Oh, yes, Father. No problem." Go, go! Get lost, will you? "We'll be fine. And if I'm sick again, I'll do it into this bucket."

Elias nods wearily, wiping his hands on the rag that's tucked into his girdle. He has a bandage around one finger, and he's limping from a scalded foot, but otherwise he seems to be in pretty good health, for a change. He isn't coughing or sweating or sniffing, and he doesn't look any more tired than usual. (His face always reminds me of a very old palliasse that's been kicked and torn and slept on and pissed on and dragged around and finally dumped in a barn, for the dogs to play with.) He moves over to Amiel's bed and pats Amiel's blanket.

"Will you be all right, Amiel?" he asks. "If anything happens, remember what I told you: horehound and tarragon in boiling water, and breathe in the steam. Hot-dry remedies for a cold-wet complaint."

Amiel nods. He's propped up against a mountain of pillows, gulping down air like a drowning man. Every breath is a major struggle: his cheeks are white, his lips blue. Elias checks his pulse and frowns a little.

"I won't be long," he repeats. "Make sure he doesn't talk, Pagan, and don't get him too excited."

"No, Father, I won't."

"Good. All right. *Dominus vobiscum.*"

And off he toddles. Weaving his way between the empty beds, through the strewing herbs, past the linen chest and the fireplace and the locked cupboard full of strange and expensive medicaments: vipers' flesh, crushed deer antlers, crabs' eyes, oil of earthworm. (I've heard all about them, from Durand.) Disappearing down the stairs.

I thought he'd never go.

"Pssst! Amiel!" Throwing off my blankets. "Are you very sick? Are you going to need me? No—wait—don't answer that. You're not supposed to talk."

Pulling my boots on; moving across to his bed. He gives me a puzzled look, but doesn't have the breath to make an inquiry. Just wheezes away like a pair of bellows with a hole in them.

"The thing is, Amiel, there's something I have to do, and I don't want anyone to know I'm doing it. So I'm going to do it now, while everyone's at Mass." God, will you look at him? Poor little beggar. Straining so hard that there's sweat on his forehead. How can I leave him like this? "But if you'd prefer me to stay, I will. Just nod, don't talk. Do you want me to stay?"

He shakes his head sluggishly. Gropes for my sleeve with one shriveled, bluish hand. "Wha'?" he mutters. "Wha're you doing?"

"I'll tell you later. Don't talk."

"Trouble?"

"No, there won't be any trouble. It's all right. If Father Elias comes back, you can tell him I was feeling better. Tell him that the medicine made me better, and I've gone back to church. Can you do that?"

Amiel nods. Good man, Amiel. You're a true friend. "Thanks for this; I won't forget it. And I'm sorry you're feeling so awful. I wish there were something I could do to help." Patting his arm, and he smiles at me. "We're all praying like mad, of course, so maybe things will improve. Let's hope so, anyway."

He nods again and has a mild coughing fit. But he won't let me hang around, just pushes me away when I try to pass him the water. Go on! Get going! Falls back exhausted as I back out of the room.

God preserve us, I hope he'll be all right. I wouldn't have left him if this errand weren't so urgent. Scuttling down the stairs and into the almonry, where the old men are huddled around a few miserable, dying embers in the fireplace. (They don't even spare me a glance.) Out the back door, into the drizzle. Turn right and right again, around the long way, to avoid the cloisters; it'll be safer if I do it like that. Slipping past the almonry, outside the herb-garden wall. Pulling my cowl down over my face. Splashing through puddles, and through the clouds of steam pouring out of my nose. God, but it's cold! Smoke drifting up from half a dozen chimneys in the abbey compound: from the almonry, the infirmary, the guesthouse, the bakery, the kitchen. Not a soul in sight.

I've never been in the guesthouse before. I know where the entrance is, but I don't know what to expect. The big carved door opens easily, on oiled hinges; there's a dim room beyond it, with torches and tables and a chest in one corner. A faint smell of whitewash mingles with the stronger scent of boiled cabbage. Everything looks clean and tidy.

Now then, where are these guests' rooms? They must be off to the right, I suppose. Through that little archway and . . . yes, here they are. Eight identical doors, opening onto a long, painted passage. Scenes from the life of Saint Martin, squeezed between the windows in the western wall: the birth of Saint Martin; Saint Martin divides his cloak with the beggar; Saint Martin founds the first Frankish monastery. (Is that a three-legged beggar, or a beggar with an oddly shaped crutch?) On the left, above the doors, are depicted the various martyrdoms of somebody — Saint George, perhaps? — who's being impaled and boiled and disemboweled, and who finally has his head chopped off.

The door underneath the beheading is slightly ajar.

"Hello?" Peering around it, cautiously. "Is anybody there?"

Whoops! There's somebody there, all right, but I don't think it's the somebody I want. Tall and well built, with a stately gray beard, an embroidered tunic and . . . ah, yes. And Raymond's turned-up nose.

"I'm sorry, my lord." (Retreating a little, as he whips around to glare at me.) "Are you Lord Bertrand?"

"I am, yes."

"Pardon, my lord, I'm looking for someone else."

Lucky Raymond. No wonder he's so proud of his father. *I'd* be proud of a father like that. Withdrawing apologetically, as he returns to his interrupted dressing. Let's just hope that his neighbor hasn't left yet.

Knock-knock-knock. My hand is shaking so much, it's hard to deliver the kind of authoritative rap on the door that announces a man of confidence. Come on, Pagan, you can do it. Stand up straight! Take a deep breath! Don't be such a miserable coward! This will only work if you get a grip on yourself.

"Come in!"

A muffled voice, low and harsh. Same accent as Aeldred's. Pushing open the door, and there he is: squat, blond, hairy, with blunt features and no neck.

Doesn't look at all like the almoner.

"What is it?" he inquires.

"Are you Father Aeldred's cousin?"

"Yes." He squints at me, frowning. "I'm Centule. Who are you?"

All right, Pagan. This is it. Nice and casual . . .

"I was looking at your horse. It's a nice horse. Did you get it with the almoner's money?"

Whew! That's done it. He looks as if he's been whacked over the ear with a lead pipe.

"*What?*" he exclaims.

"Shh!" Closing the door behind me. "Not so loud. If you raise your voice, you can be heard in the next room."

"What is this?"

"Don't worry, I won't tell. It'll be our little secret: yours, mine, and the almoner's."

"Get out!" (He's beginning to sweat already.) "Get out of here!"

"You mean you want me to go to the Abbot and tell him what I heard? Because I will, you know."

"What—what you heard?"

Ha! That's done it. He sits down abruptly, on the unmade bed, as if his knees have given way. He might look tough on the outside, but his guts are made of wet feathers.

"What do you mean?" he says.

"I was in the next room. I heard you shouting— you and the almoner. The walls are quite thin."

"That's nonsense," he says, trying to assume a carefree tone. "Get along with you, boy. I'm too busy for these silly games."

"The Abbot won't think it's a game. Not if I tell him. The Abbot will expel the almoner, and then you won't get your money anymore."

Watching him closely, as his eyes go blank. I'm

taking a big risk here. A real leap in the dark. Who knows what this money business is all about? It might be quite harmless. It might be a legitimate debt.

On the other hand, it might not be.

"What do you want?" he says, in a harsh voice . . . and suddenly it hits me.

I've pulled it off. I've won. I set the trap, and he fell straight in.

This is unbelievable.

"I'll tell you what I want, Master Centule. I want you to tell me the whole story, from beginning to end." (Arranging my words with care, to conceal the fact that I don't even know where the story starts, let alone where it finishes.) "I want to know every detail."

"Why?"

"Because it's worth money!" Trying to sound impatient. Oh, it's like spearing fish in a barrel; I can't believe I was ever nervous about this. "If the almoner pays *you*, then he'll certainly pay me. Just to keep the Abbot from finding out about this whole shady business."

A thoughtful grunt, but he still seems uncertain. Time to take the biggest gamble of all. Please, God, please—don't let him call my bluff.

"And then, of course, there's Father Montazin . . ."

"Oh, all right, all right, I'll tell you!" He wipes the sweat from his brow with short, stubby fingers. "I'll tell you, and then you can get out. What do you want to know?"

What do I want to know? Good question. "Let's start with you. Are you and Aeldred really related?"

A snort.

"To that worm? Not likely."

"So you met—"

"We met at Voutenay-sur-Cure. We were both monks there. He was the child-master, which is how he managed to molest all those boys."

Sweet saints preserve us. You mean—you mean—

"I didn't know anything about it," he continues, "not until the last boy reported him. And then of course he disappeared—escaped in the night, before they could pass sentence. No one knew where he'd gone, until I happened to turn up here." A sly smirk becomes visible through the undergrowth on his chin. "It was the hand of God, I believe."

"How did you end up here, though?"

"Oh, I was looking for help." Another unsavory smirk. "Things weren't going too well, after I was thrown—I mean, after I left—Voutenay. I was down on my luck, and wandering around. Stopped in at the almonry, here, to pick up a bite to eat. And who should I see but old Aeldred?" This time he laughs—a savage, spiteful laugh. "He almost died on the spot when I walked in. But we came to an agreement."

God save us. I think I'm going to be sick. But I mustn't get angry; I mustn't let it show. Keep calm, Pagan. Keep a lid on it.

"What about Montazin? How did he get involved?"

"As far as I know, Montazin found out from the guest-master. What's his name? Sicard? Nasty little drooling baldy who listens at doors. Montazin got him the job: I believe they're cousins."

So that's it. Aeldred's being blackmailed; Sicard overhears; Sicard tells Montazin; Montazin uses that information to make Aeldred do . . . what? Embezzle more money? Deliver it to Lady Beatrice? Anything and everything, just to keep Montazin quiet.

"If you're looking to get much out of Aeldred," Centule adds, "you're out of luck. He says he's already at the breaking point, the sniveling toad. That's why we were arguing."

"I don't want very much. Just enough to pay off a girl."

"Well, don't say I didn't warn you." His face settles into a sullen, ugly expression, in which distrust battles with resentment and fatigue. "Is that all? Are you finished? Because I've got to be going."

"Where are you living, anyway? In Carcassonne?"

"That's none of your business." He stands up. "Now get out of here. And if I see you again, I'll beat your head to a bloody pulp."

Temper, temper. Some people don't have any self-control. "Thanks for your time, Centule. And don't worry—I won't tell Aeldred that you're the one who told me. I'm not that sort of monk."

Waving cheerfully as I make my departure, just to annoy him. Closing the door softly on his dawning look of indignation.

Oh, Pagan. What can I say? You are *magnificent*!

✞CHAPTER TWENTY-ONE✞

I can't stop thinking about Brother Macharius, back at Saint Joseph's. I must have been—what? Seven? Eight? And little Lambert was only about six. I remember what he was like when he arrived, always asking questions and running around, laughing at the picture of the pigs in Saint Stephen's chapel. And then he changed, just like that. Stopped laughing. Stopped running. Hid in corners during the day and wet the bed at night. Of course, we all knew what was happening: it had happened once or twice before. But we didn't say a word, not to anyone. Too scared, I suppose. Scared and confused.

And that kind of stuff is always going on in monasteries; you hear about it all the time. All those dirty jokes about lifting a monk's skirts . . . I mean, everyone knows about it. Everyone. Why do you think monks aren't allowed to talk to oblates? Or touch them? Or sit next to them? It's to stop the bad monks from molesting children.

Doesn't help, though. Not if your own child-master is a pederast. God, I wish I'd spoken up. Why was I such a coward? It could have been me, in that bell tower with Macharius. Pure luck that it wasn't. But instead of doing something, I just—in God's name, I just pretended it didn't happen! How could I have done that? How could I have been such a miserable, crawling, weak-kneed, paltry, pathetic . . .

But it won't happen this time. Oh, no. I'm going to get that son of Belial, the way I should have gotten Macharius. I'm going to get him and Montazin and Sicard and all that verminous scum, just as soon as I have some proof. Proof, proof! No one will believe me without proof. And Centule won't talk, not to the Abbot. Oh, if *only* the Abbot were here. Even without proof, I might have sown a seed of doubt in his mind. But then again, I probably wouldn't have been allowed anywhere near him.

"Herrem . . . Gherlerriumbemm—"

Raymond, talking in his sleep. I wonder what

time it is. Haven't slept a wink since we went to bed. How slowly the night crawls by when you're lying awake worrying. Not that there's any reason to worry about Centule: he'll never say a word to Aeldred about this, I'm sure of it. He'll scurry back to his lair and keep his head down for another month, hoping that Aeldred and I will sort it out between ourselves. What a cockroach he is. Doesn't surprise me that they threw him out of Voutenay-sur-Cure. The question is, what did he do to deserve expulsion? Did he steal? Cheat? Vandalize? Probably all three, to judge from what he's doing now. Oh, God, I'm so exhausted. Why can't I get to sleep?

Sudden noise from across the room: the creak of someone shifting his weight in bed. Look around, and it's Roland. He sits up, pushes his blankets off, swings his feet to the floor. Seems to be looking for his chamber pot.

No. On second thought, he's not looking for his chamber pot. He's looking for his boots. What in God's name is he doing? Surely he can't be going outside? Watching as he stands up slowly, his face expressionless in the soft glow of the candle.

Waiting until he's slipped out the door.

Quick! Get up! Get after him! Can I make it without my boots? Perhaps not. Yanking them on with fumbling fingers; holding my breath on the way past Clement's snores. It's as cold as the devil's heart outside, and black as the smoke of sin, but I can hear Roland's shuffling footsteps along the path to the refectory. They begin to sound hollow as he turns into the covered passage. Quick, quick! Don't let him escape!

"*Roland.*"

It's just a little squeak, from the back of my throat, but he hears me. The footsteps come to a halt.

"*It's me, Pagan!*"

Still not a sound. Feeling my way along the wall of the monks' dormitory, until it suddenly disappears. (Must have reached the corner.) Groping through space with one outstretched hand, in search of something warm and soft. Where are you, Roland? Where are you hiding? You've got to be in here — I heard you a moment ago.

Yike!

"Shh!" It's his voice, his hands. Almost scared me to death. "What are you doing?" he whispers.

"What are *you* doing?"

"I'm going to the church. To pray."

"At this hour?"

"Go back to bed, Pagan."

"No."

"Pagan—"

"We have to talk. It's time we had a talk."

"We can talk tomorrow."

"No, we can't! How can we, when we never have a moment to ourselves?"

"But the circator—"

"Oh, I see. So you're scared of the big bad circator, are you?"

A long silence. That's done it. I can hear his heavy breathing, as his grip tightens on my arm.

"Very well," he says, "but we can't stay here."

"I know that. Just follow me."

We'll be safe outside the herb garden: all we have to do is get to that door opposite the stables. Taking his hand (which is ice-cold) and dragging him back toward our dormitory, step by step, until the rough stone wall yields to smooth wood. Must be the door to the oblates' room. And here's our room, and if we keep to this path we'll be there before you know it.

Aha! What did I tell you? More wood, roughened by the weather. A cold, metal stud. A rattling bar.

"Help me with this, will you?" Softly, over my shoulder.

"It's barred on the inside."

He gropes his way past me; finds what he's looking for. There's a scraping sound as he lifts the heavy, oaken beam.

"I think I'll hold on to this," he whispers. "If I don't, we'll never find it again. You go first. Be careful."

Oh, I'll be careful, Roland, don't you worry. Fumbling around in the darkness; finding the door; pulling it open. The cold wind hits me as I squeeze through the gap. Ouch! My head!

"Sorry," he murmurs. (Must have hit me with the beam.) "Where are you? Pagan?"

"I'm here. Down here."

"Move over."

Shuffling to one side, obediently. Feeling the cold biting into my ankles. But his warm bulk slides down the wall, and now he's beside me, blowing on his hands. Crouching there in silence.

Waiting for me to start.

"What's wrong with you, my lord?"

"Don't call me that."

"What's wrong with you, Roland?"

"There's nothing wrong."

"Oh, really? You don't eat, you don't speak, you wander around at night like a cockroach—"

"I told you, I was going to the church—"

"To pray? What for? An appetite?"

No response.

"You're fading away, Roland. You're fading away in front of my eyes, and you tell me there's nothing wrong!"

"I'm fasting."

"You're *what*?"

"Shh! Not so loud."

"But it's not Lent! Why should you be fasting?"

"I'm fasting in penance."

Sweet saints preserve us. In penance? I've never heard such rubbish. "Penance for what?"

"For my sins."

Your *what*? Oh, please, this is ludicrous. You wouldn't know a sin if it came up and wiped its nose all over your scapular. "And what sins would these be?"

Silence.

"You'd better tell me, Roland."

Still nothing. God damn you, Roland. God damn you for your stupid, stuck-up, solitary, stiff-necked pride.

"If you don't tell me . . ." (Trying to keep my

voice steady.) "If you don't tell me right now, I'm going to walk out of this place and I'm never coming back."

"Pagan—"

"Do you think I'm going to sit here and watch you starve yourself to death? Watch you shrivel away to nothing?"

"You don't understand—"

"Why are you doing this?"

"Because I loved a heretic!" It bursts out of him, like juice out of a grape. But he quickly lowers his voice again. "I loved a heretic," he repeats. "That's why."

"You mean Esclaramonde?"

A slight movement. (A nod?) This is crazy. I don't understand. "But you weren't even a monk then!"

"She was a heretic."

"So what? She was still a good woman."

"No." It comes out as a strangled squawk. "No, I . . . No . . ."

"Roland, this is crazy. Are you crazy? I knew her as well as you did. Of course she was a good woman. If she hadn't been, you wouldn't have loved her."

"Stop it. Stop it, Pagan, please." His words sound

muffled, as if he's talking through his hands. "She was a heretic. She—she endangered my immortal soul and defiled my house with her corruption—"

"Wait. Hold it right there." Now I've got it. Now I understand. "Who have you been talking to?"

Harsh breathing.

"Roland? Who have you been talking to? I know you've been talking to someone—"

"Father Guilabert."

"Guilabert?"

"You don't—"

"That fat sod? That pompous tub of lard? I don't believe it!"

"He is our Father Superior—"

"He is a pile of snot in the shape of a man! He has a brain the size of a pimple! What the hell did you listen to him for? He wouldn't know his arse from his armpit!"

"Oh, but *you* are so well informed! *You* can solve everyone's problems!" He spits it out in the querulous, high-pitched tones of an angry scullion.

I've never heard him talk like this. It's weird. It's frightening.

"This may come as a surprise to you, Pagan, but you're not the world's expert on everything, no matter what you believe!"

"I didn't say I was—"

"You're not even a monk!"

"Well, neither are you!"

"I know, I know that. But I'm going to be." All of a sudden, he's quiet again. Subdued. Intense. "I'm going to be a monk," he whispers, "and I'm going to find God. I'm going to find a path. I *must* find a path. It's my last chance here."

"Roland—"

"I must, I must, I must!"

And the bells start to ring. Wouldn't you know it? What terrible timing.

"Nocturnes!" Roland hisses.

"I know. Get up."

"What are we—?"

"You go straight to church. Say you've been praying. I'll go to the latrines and say I had the flux."

"But—"

"Hurry! Quick! Run!"

Hell in a handcart. It's a good thing somebody's still using his head around here.

✝ CHAPTER TWENTY-TWO ✝

"Silence, novices! Silence, please!"

Clement tries to clap his hands, but only manages to produce a weak little noise like the last gasp of a drowning piglet. (His knuckles are so swollen these days that he can't even straighten his fingers properly.)

"What do you think you're doing, Bernard?" he exclaims. "It's your turn to arrange the stools. Fetch the Bible, Raymond. Durand, I've told you before: if you're going to wipe your nose, do it on your sleeve, not on your hand. Hands are for touching books. Pagan—over here."

Groan. Looks like another private session for yours truly. Must be something to do with this enormous hulking book he's making me drag around.

It's even bigger than Boethius.

"Sit down, all of you. Whose turn is it to read? Is it yours, Bernard?"

"No, Master, it's Amiel's."

"Oh, I see. Well, since Amiel is still sick, we'll let Gaubert do it. He needs the practice."

Poor old Gaubert. Look at his face! You'd think he'd been asked to chew a tunnel through a dung heap.

"John Chapter Ten, please, Gaubert," the Toothless Terror continues. "And I want you all to listen carefully, because I'll be asking questions on that chapter when he's done. Not you, Pagan, I have something else for you to read. Come here."

Give ear to my prayer, O God, and hide not thyself from my supplication. Don't tell me I'm actually going to have to *read* this monster. I think I'd rather be hit over the head with it.

"This book," says Clement, grimacing as he lowers himself onto a stool, "is a very wonderful book called *Ad Herrenium de arte rhetorica.* It was written by Marcus Tullius Cicero, the great orator and philospher, and it concerns the art of rhetoric. Now, what did Boethius say about rhetoric?"

217

Pause. Oh—sorry. Am I supposed to answer that? I thought it was a rhetorical question.

"Pagan?" (He's starting to get that rasp in his voice.) "What did Boethius say—"

"He said that rhetoric has three species."

"Which are?"

"Judicial, deliberative, and . . ." Um. God, what was the other one? I've completely forgotten.

"Iudicale, deliberativum, and demonstrativum."

Demonstrativum! Of course. You took the words right out of my mouth. Over on the other side of the dormitory, Gaubert is stumbling through the verse about the man that entereth not by the door into the sheepfold, and it's kind of distracting.

"Yes," Clement growls, stoically ignoring Gaubert's crippled pronunciation, "those are indeed the three kinds of cases that an orator must undertake. But what are the five things that he must possess? Can you tell me that?"

Of course I can. "Invention, arrangement, expression, memorization, delivery."

"Correct. *Inventio, dispositio, elocutio, memoria, pronuntiatio.* This book is a profound study of these things, and of the various divisions of speech, and of the elements of style possessed by all great orators. Orators and letter-writers." With trembling hands he takes the book from my grasp, and almost drops it. "There is also a very interesting section here on rhetorical composition, which is made up of the *salutatio*, the *benevolentiae captatio*, the *narratio*, the *petitio*, and the *conclusio*. Yes, Durand, what is it?"

Durand has sidled up like a beaten dog, all pleading eyes and hunched shoulders. A bad cold has turned his little snub nose into something resembling a squashed grape. He stands there, moon-faced and slack-jawed, breathing through an open mouth.

"Please, Master," he snuffles, "I want to go to the latrines."

Clement gives vent to an exasperated sigh. "Very well," he snarls. "But don't dawdle."

"No, Master. Thank you, Master."

As Durand turns to leave, it suddenly hits me. This could be my chance. Quick, Pagan, cross your legs! Bite your lip! Wriggle around! You have to look convincing.

"Please, Master, can I go, too?" (Trying to force the sweat through my skin.) "I need to go, too."

"You?" he snaps. "Don't talk nonsense."

"But I need to." Whine, whine. "I think I've got the flux. I can't concentrate. I'll soil my drawers—"

"Oh, all right, go!" (Hurrah!) "But if you're not back before Gaubert reaches the eighteenth verse, Pagan, I'll have the skin off your back."

Skin? What skin? That's been taken off already. Hurrying after Durand, who's waddling up the path as fast as his pudgy legs can carry him, sniffing and coughing and wiping his nose. Past the herb garden. Around the corner. Into the covered passage.

"Durand! Wait!"

He stops and turns his head. Stuck into his doughy face—with its dribbling nose and double chin and slack bottom lip—is a pair of big, round, rather pensive dark eyes that look a bit incongruous in that face, like the proverbial jewel of gold in the swine's snout. They're the sort of eyes that always seem to be hanging about at the edge of things, watching.

He blinks them at me in a startled fashion.

"What?" he says.

"There's something I have to ask you." (Quietly.) "Not here, though. Wait until we get to the latrines."

"What is it?"

"I'll tell you in the latrines."

The best thing about the latrines in this monastery is that they actually work. Whoever designed the drainage ought to be sanctified: summer or winter, rain or shine, there's never a nasty pileup in the sluice. I've seen latrines—I've even *cleaned* latrines—that would make a leper vomit. But this isn't one of them.

Of course, the disadvantage of having presentable latrines is that people tend to linger inside them. I've heard of one monk, long since dead, who actually used to sit in here and read. Today, however, it's much too cold to expose anything for long: the only occupant is pulling up his drawers just as we cross the threshold.

"Dominus vobiscum," he mutters. In the dimness you can just make out his gleaming scalp, his huge hands, his wet black eyes and pendulous lower lip. It's Sicard, the guest-master.

"Benedictus sit Dominus, Pater." Malodorous maggot. I hope he's got the flux. Waiting until he's shuffled out before I tackle Durand.

"Listen, Durand, can I ask you something?"

"Of course. What is it?"

"Shh! Not too loud." (Our voices seem to echo around the damp, cavernous space.) "I don't want anyone to hear this."

"Hear what?"

221

"Well . . ." How shall I put it? "Has the almoner ever—has he ever—well, bothered you?"

"Bothered me?"

"You know." Or do you? He's staring at me with those big, startled eyes, and it's hard to discern just how much is hidden behind them. "Has he ever kissed you, or patted you, or—or—"

"Raped me, you mean?"

Well, I'll be spit-roasted. "Um . . . yes, I suppose that is what I mean."

"Oh, no, he's never raped me. Why? Has he raped you?"

"No." What a laugh. Here I was, wondering how much he knew, when of course he knows the whole thing. How could he avoid it? He's in a monastery, for God's sake.

He wipes his nose and peers at me from under his fringe of fine, lank hair. "Has he raped someone else, then?"

"I don't know." Fighting the insane urge to giggle. "I don't know, has he?"

"I don't think so." When Durand frowns, he looks much older. "No one's said anything to me. I didn't even know he *liked* boys."

"Well, he does."

"How did you figure that out?"

"I just did."

"But how?"

Oh, Lord, and now he wants the whole story. Somehow I knew he would.

"Please, Pagan, I won't tell, I promise." His breath smells of the thyme he's been eating as a cold cure. He's practically wagging his tail. "I know how to keep a secret. You can trust me. I'd never tell on you, never. Have I ever told on you?"

"No, but—"

"Please. I know there's something going on; I've been watching you. Why won't you trust anyone? I know a lot of things that other people don't know. Maybe I can help."

Maybe you can, at that. You'd certainly be the first person around here who's ever tried. But do you really want to help? Or do you just want a juicy bit of gossip?

It's his hand that really convinces me. The way he pats my arm, so hesitant, so earnest, as if he's afraid that I'll bite him. He glances toward the entrance, but there's no one in sight. No sound of footsteps in the cloisters. Just the drip-drip-drip of water in the sluice.

Perhaps I should risk it.

"Remember that cousin of Aeldred's? The one who visits every month?" Waiting until he's nodded. "Well, I talked to the cousin yesterday, and he told me Aeldred used to be a monk in a Burgundian monastery. But then he left, because they found out he was molesting the oblates."

"No!"

"Yes. And I'm sure it's true, because Aeldred is paying this cousin money. To keep him quiet."

"Paying him money? I don't understand. What money?"

"Money that he's stolen. Alms money."

Durand's jaw drops. It's not a pretty sight.

"The trouble is, I don't have any proof. And without proof, no one's going to believe me."

The words are hardly out of my mouth before Durand blushes. Even in this light, you can see the wash of red that engulfs his face.

"*I* believe you," he croaks.

"Well—good. At least someone does." Better get moving, I suppose, before Clement comes screaming in like the Beast of the Apocalypse. Hoisting up my skirt. Preparing to aim.

"Pagan?"

Tinkle, tinkle.

"What?"

Another pause. Go on, Durand. Whatever it is, just say it. He takes a deep breath.

"I know you didn't bring that girl in," he announces.

God preserve us! Good thing I'm finished, or I would have pissed up the wall.

"You *what*?"

"I saw her with Roquefire one night. She was Roquefire's girl." He's staring at his feet. "I saw her in the kitchens."

"You saw her?" I can't believe it. "What were you doing?"

This time the blush is so deep, it's almost purple.

"I was stealing food," he whispers.

Stealing food. In the kitchens. And he saw her! He actually saw her, with Roquefire! "But why didn't you say something?" In God's name, Durand! "I got beaten for that! Why didn't you tell them?"

"I couldn't." There's a crack in his voice. "How could I tell them what I'd been doing? They would have beaten *me*."

That's true. They would have. And it might not have done any good.

Still and all . . .

"I'm sorry, Pagan." He's wiping his eyes now, as well as his nose. "I'm sorry I'm such a coward. It's terrible, what happened to you."

"Never mind. You're not to blame." He isn't, either: he's only a child. How can you expect a child to speak up when he's scared witless? Poor little scrap. He's not the right shape to be a hero. "Cheer up, Durand—I'm not angry. At least I know that you can keep your mouth shut. You will keep your mouth shut, won't you? About the almoner? He mustn't know that I know."

"All right." He's frowning again. "But aren't you going to tell the others?"

The others? "What others?"

"The rest of us. You know. Bernard and Raymond and—"

"Raymond!" Ha! "Do you think Raymond would listen to a word I say?"

"He likes you, you know."

"*Raymond?*"

"He does. He admires you." The round, dark eyes haven't left my face. "He's just jealous, that's all. So is everyone. So am I. But then I've got more reason to be."

Jealous? Don't make me laugh. You might as well be jealous of a gumboil. "Oh, right. Sure.

226

Naturally. Why not be jealous of the way I'm kicked around? It's an enviable thing, being the official whipping post."

Durand smiles and shakes his head. It's an odd little smile, but then again, when you think about it, he's an odd little person. I never realized that until now.

"You're very clever, Pagan," he says, "but sometimes you can be a bit stupid, if you don't mind my saying so." He shuffles his feet, looking over his shoulder. "I think we'd better be getting back now. If we don't, Father Clement will be down on us like the church roof."

Amen to that. And we both know who'll be getting the worst of it.

✠CHAPTER TWENTY-THREE✠

"Hello, Amiel." Clement stands at the foot of the bed, leaning on his walking stick. "How are you today? You look better."

Amiel nods. He does look better: there's a little more pink in his face, and a little less blue. But his chest is still heaving away desperately.

"I'm much better now," he gasps. "Father Elias said that I can get up soon."

"I said nothing of the sort," Elias objects. "I said that if you continue to improve, we might sit you in a chair next week. That's all I said."

"Brother Elias tells me that you're strong enough to be visited." Clement's voice is hoarser than usual, thanks to the highly epidemic nature of

Durand's cold. He looks as if he's been killed, buried, and dug up again—a tottering wreck just barely able to support himself. His crippled hands are wrapped in fur mittens. "He tells me that you want to see your friends."

"Yes, Master." Cough. Wheeze. I feel as if I've wandered into a hospice. Nothing but clogged chests and runny noses as far as the eye can see. Even Roland doesn't look too good, with his drawn, shadowy face. But then again, it's his own damned fault. So it's hard to be sympathetic.

"I have to go to chapter now," Clement continues. "If I leave you here with your friends, Amiel, will you promise to be good and quiet, and not to overexcite yourself?"

"Oh, yes, Master. Yes. Oh, yes."

Sounds a bit overexcited already. Clement gives him a skeptical look and turns to address the rest of us.

"Brother Elias will not be going to chapter," he declares, "because Brother Landric over there is too sick to leave. Consequently, if there is any rowdy behavior, I will most certainly hear about it when I return. Do I make myself clear, Pagan?"

Oh, come on. Why are you always picking on me? Every time I break wind, I get my ear chewed off.

"Do I make myself clear?"

By the bouncing balls of Beelzebub. "Master, you always make yourself clear. It's your rhetorical training."

He narrows his eyes and points his stick in my direction. It looks as if he's going to give me one of his pokes, but without the support of the walking stick his knees can't take the pressure. They buckle, and he has to grab at Brother Elias—who mutters something in Latin about going to bed.

"Rubbish!" Clement snarls. And he straightens his back before stomping off toward the stairs, just to show everyone that he's perfectly capable of looking after himself.

Elias shakes his head a little.

"All right, boys," he says (apparently unaware of the fact that Roland, at least, hasn't been a boy for some considerable time). "I want you to remember that Brother Landric is very ill, and we don't want to make him any worse. So no shouting, please, or laughing, or running around."

Laughing? Shouting? Running around? I've forgotten what they are, let alone how to do them. Elias gives Amiel a pat on the wrist before returning to Brother Landric, who's twitching and sweating at the other end of the infirmary.

There's a funny smell in the air.

"You can sit on the bed," Amiel wheezes as we cluster around. "It doesn't matter."

"How are you feeling?" (Raymond.) "Are you really feeling better?"

"Oh, yes."

"We would have brought you something to eat," Gaubert chimes in, "but Durand ate it."

A burst of laughter, quickly stifled by the look that Elias flings at us from across the room. Amiel takes Gaubert's hand.

"So what's been going on?" he inquires weakly.

"Well . . . everyone's got a cold," says Raymond, "and it's all Durand's fault."

"It is not!"

"Even the prior has it, and every time he sneezes he wobbles all over the place like a big fat wineskin."

More muffled laughter. Bernard sits on the bed.

"It's freezing outside," he remarks. "You're lucky to be in here all day."

"No, I'm not."

"Yes, you are. If you sit down in the latrines, your arse freezes to the seat. They have to chip you off."

"It snowed last night," Raymond adds. "Did you know about that?"

"Yes, Father Elias told me."

"And the well froze, so they're melting ice in the kitchens." Raymond sighs, and looks at Bernard. "Do you remember what it was like in Carcassonne, when we used to go skating? I'd love to go skating."

Skating? "What's skating?"

All eyes focus on me. There's a long pause. Everyone waits for Raymond to reply.

"Don't you know what skating is?" he says. "You put wooden things on your feet and glide over the ice very fast."

"How fast?"

"Oh, as fast as a horse. Faster."

"Really?" That's incredible. "But don't you fall down?"

Bernard snickers. "He falls down, all right. He was always falling down."

"Not as much as you, Bernard."

"Father Aeldred fell down," Amiel says abruptly. "He slipped on the ice, and he came in here because he thought he'd broken his ankle. But he hadn't." As everyone digests this piece of news, Amiel leans forward and adds, in a low voice, "I don't like him very much."

"Why not?" The question is out of Durand's mouth before I've even opened mine. "He hasn't messed with you, has he?"

Oh, God. That's done it. There's a puzzled silence, followed by an exchange of meaningful glances. Durand turns bright red.

It's Raymond, once again, who takes the initiative.

"What do you mean?" he says in hushed tones. He leans forward, his eyes bright with interest. "Do you mean like little Enguerrand and that disgusting gardener?"

Durand appears to have lost the power of speech. He wriggles uncomfortably and casts me a hunted look. God damn you, Durand, you and your big mouth! I told you it was a secret!

"He didn't mess with *you*, did he?" Raymond prompts, his head almost touching Durand's.

Suddenly everyone's huddled together, like cows under a tree in the rain. Only Ademar and Roland stand apart: Ademar because he's simply not interested, and Roland—well, I don't think Roland's quite grasped what's going on. He doesn't have the monastic background to pick up those all-important nuances.

"What did he do to you, Durand?" It's obvious that Raymond's not going to let Durand off the hook. Poor old Durand, caught between the rocks and the reef. Doesn't want to upset either of us.

Probably time for me to step in.

"He didn't do anything."

Heads turn; jaws drop. Raymond peers at me intently.

"Do you know about this?" he demands, putting a great deal of force into a very soft whisper. "Don't tell me he messed with *you*."

"No. But he was thrown out of another monastery for molesting children."

You could hear a sparrow fart.

Bernard's the first to recover.

"He *what*?"

"Shhh!" (Keep it down!) "Do you want Father Elias to hear?"

"That's rubbish." Raymond, angrily. "How could you possibly know a thing like that?"

"Because I heard it from the man who's blackmailing him."

There. That's done the trick. It's deprived him of breath, like a kick in the rib cage. And with Raymond winded, Amiel has a chance to speak.

"Blackmailing who?" he gasps. "Is Father Aeldred blackmailing someone?"

"No." Bog-brain. "Someone's blackmailing him . . . the man who calls himself Aeldred's cousin. The one who was asking him for money. He's not Aeldred's cousin at all, he's a former monk from the Burgundian monastery where Aeldred used to live."

"Lies," says Raymond. "All lies." But his delivery is rather weak, as if he's lost most of his stuffing. "You're always trying to blame the monks. You tried to blame them when you let that girl in—"

"No, he didn't." Durand doesn't even let him finish the sentence. "Pagan didn't let that girl in. Roquefire let her in."

Raymond snorts.

"He did, I tell you! That girl was Roquefire's girl. I've seen them together before, in the kitchen."

"In the kitchen? When?"

Durand blushes. "When I—when I was getting something to eat," he stammers, whereupon Bernard rolls his eyes.

But before he can say anything, Raymond turns back to me with an intent, guarded, quizzical look on his face. It's a look that I've never seen there before. A look that really suits him.

"If you know all this," he says softly, "why haven't you told any of the monks?"

"Because they won't believe him!" Durand breaks in. "Not without proof. They'll think he's lying, the way you did. He needs proof, or it won't work."

Thanks, Durand, but I'll speak for myself if you don't mind. Glancing over to where Elias is sitting, spooning milk down Landric's throat. Let's hope he hasn't heard any of this.

"Pagan." It's Roland. He's hovering at the edge of the group, and he sounds exhausted. "You—you should have told me. Why didn't you?"

Why didn't I tell you? I like that! What a gall you have, standing there and—and—sweet saints preserve us! Are you trying to make me feel *guilty*? First cast the beam out of thine own eye, Roland!

"Well, I don't know." Glaring up at him. "I don't know, Roland, maybe I had to tell somebody else first."

He blinks, just once, and I know I've hit the target. His face is blank, his eyes are blank, but I know. It's something about the way he becomes very still.

"Pagan." Gaubert tugs at my sleeve. "Why don't you get some proof? Then they'd believe you."

"It's not that easy." (Durand shoves his oar in again.) "What kind of proof can you get? Aeldred won't admit to anything. The man who's black-mailing him won't admit to anything, either."

"Except perhaps in confession," says Bernard, "but that's no good."

"Maybe we could trick them, somehow," Amiel croaks, and Bernard turns on him scornfully.

"How?"

"I'm—I'm not sure . . ."

"Big help you are, Amiel."

Wait! Hold on, now! This is going too fast. Looking around at the circle of eager faces: at Gaubert, brimming with enthusiasm; at Bernard, frowning thoughtfully; at Amiel, restless and worried; at Raymond . . .

At Raymond. Even as our gazes meet, it flashes into my head—the perfect solution—and he's thought of it, too, I can tell. It's there in his eyes, and he beats me to it.

"A letter," he says, before I get the chance. A letter. Of course. It's so obvious, and yet . . . well, I never could have sent one myself, could I? I don't know a soul outside this monastery, I don't know anyone who might be traveling north.

But Raymond does.

"I could write a letter to the Abbot of that monastery Aeldred came from," he murmurs. "I'm always writing letters to my mother."

Yes, by God. "So you'll be able to get the ink and the parchment—"

"And I'll call myself Brother Raymond." (He's getting excited now.) "I'll ask for the whole story. What Aeldred did. What he looks like. Everything. And then," he finishes, "I could give the letter to my father, to pass on to one of his friends. They're always moving around."

Oh, Raymond. You cluster of camphire in the vineyards of Engedi. I could kiss you. "Brilliant! Wonderful! What a brilliant idea, Raymond! You're a genius."

He smiles at that. It's not a superior smile at all: it's a shy, reluctant, exhilarated smile. He rubs his nose in an effort to hide it.

"The trouble is, I don't know how long you might have to wait for an answer," he warns me. "It may be weeks before any of my father's friends go to Burgundy. And then it may be months before the Abbot's reply gets back to him. You could be waiting until next summer."

238

That's all right, my friend. I've waited this long; I can afford to wait a bit more. I just need to know that someday, somehow, I'm going to see Montazin's little conspiracy crushed like a louse under the heel of my boot.

CHAPTER TWENTY-FOUR

Where's Raymond? Why doesn't he come back? Won't his father take the letter? What's he *doing* in there?

"Pagan!"

Oh, leave me alone, you old snakeskin.

"Pagan, you're not concentrating. Look at me. Pagan! What is *brevitas*?"

Brevitas. Brevitas. Brief—oh, no, I remember. "It's rapidity of narration."

"And *continuato*?"

Continuato. That's a hard one. Let's see . . . Wait. Are those footsteps? Raymond's footsteps?

"Pagan!" Clement drives his stick into the floor. "Are you still asleep? Have you left your brain in bed? Look at me!"

Look at you? Why would I want to look at you? You look like the husk of a beetle that's been eaten out by ants. Sniffing and shaking and coughing in that disgusting fashion. . . . It's enough to make anyone sick.

God. How cold I am.

"What is *continuato*?" He just goes on and on, like an attack of the flux. "Pagan? Answer me."

"It's a rapid succession of words completing a sentence."

"*Dubitatio*?"

"An assumed hesitation."

"*Descriptio*?"

"A description of someone's personal appearance."

"*No!*" This time the Terror's voice is so loud that Bernard stops reading, startled and apprehensive. Clement glares across the room.

"Did I tell you to stop, Bernard?"

"No, Master—"

"Then continue. Ignore what's going on over here, it's none of your concern."

Obediently, Bernard drops his gaze to the psalter in front of him. When he begins to read again, his breath comes out in damp and filmy jets of steam. The rest of them sit huddled in fur-lined cloaks, their hands tucked under their armpits.

241

"Pagan! Look here! What's the matter with you? Are you sick? Are you drunk? Did you hit yourself on the head this morning?" Clement reaches over and prods me in the chest. "Something must be wrong. A child could have answered that question. I can't believe that a person so puffed up with intellectual conceit—"

"Descriptio." (You slug-faced scum-bucket.) "'A clear and impressive statement of the results of an action.'"

So there. Clement snorts and opens his mouth to speak, but before he can deliver his next batch of insults, someone appears on the threshold: someone who stands there with snow on his shoulders, cheeks red with cold, gray eyes sparkling. Someone who looks at me and winks.

It's Raymond.

"Well, Raymond," says Clement, "what took you so long? You can join the others now."

"Yes, Master."

"And kindly don't drip on the book, if you please, or I'll wring you out myself."

Come on, Raymond. Did you do it? Did he take it? Give me a sign! You said you'd give me a sign! Watching him cross the room, with a skip and a saunter, his curls bobbing with each frisky step.

As he sits down beside Roland, he kisses the back of his hand at me.

Yes! He did it! Hooray! It worked! God, what a relief. Bless the Lord, O my soul, and all that is within me, bless His holy name.

"Pagan."

By the boiling bowels of Baal. Turning to meet the flinty gaze of the Terror, who looks exactly like Death on a Pale Horse with Hell following unto him. Even his voice sounds deadly.

"It appears that your mind is on other things," he says. "Perhaps my questions aren't difficult enough to engage your mighty intellect. Perhaps they're giving you room to reflect on other matters—on things unholy and unchaste."

Oh, please. Give it a rest, will you? How can anyone be unchaste in this weather?

"What you need," Clement continues, "is a challenge. Something suitably formidable. Something to cut your teeth on." He stares down at the floor, thinking so energetically that the veins stand out on his temples. (With any luck his brain will burst.)

Rolling my eyes at Raymond, who starts making signs at me with the fluid skill of a lifetime's practice: *letter—go—twelve—days* . . . What does it mean

243

when you put all your fingers together on your forehead?

Suddenly Clement breaks the silence.

"Te rogamus ut nobis parcas, ut nobis indulgeas, ut ad veram poenitentiam nos perducere digneris."

Pardon? Staring at him, open-mouthed. He makes an impatient noise and begins to repeat himself.

"Te rogamus ut nobis parcas . . ."

Oh, I see. Well, if you want a translation, why don't you ask for one? Let's think, now. *Te rogamus . . .* "'We beseech you that you would spare us, that you would pardon us, that you would bring us to true penance.'"

"Correct." He nods. "And what rhetorical device is illustrated in that sentence?"

Help! What *rhetorical device?* Sweet saints preserve us.

"Come on, Pagan—"

"Repetitio!"

"Which is?"

"'The repetition of the same word at the beginning of each clause.'"

A grunt from Clement. I suppose that means I've got it right. Why the hell can't he scare up a compliment occasionally?

"*Quid mihi est in caelo?*" he says.

Quid mihi est in caelo? That's easy. "'Whom else have I in heaven?'"

"And what can you find in that sentence?"

"*Ratiocinatio.*"

"Which is?"

"'A question addressed to oneself.'"

"Correct. *Totum huius capitis corpus, etsi diversae facies, in posterioribus tamen non discrepat.*"

Oof! That's a hard one. Let's see. The whole body . . . No. All the followers of this chief, although their faces are diverse . . . *in posterioribus?* What's that? Oh, I see. Very amusing. Remind me to stitch up my sides.

"'All the followers of this chief, although their faces are diverse, do not differ in what comes after them.' An example of *adnominatio.*" There! Got it. Once again he nods.

"Correct," he declares. "And what is *adnominatio?*"

"A pun." (If you can call it that.) "At least, it's supposed to be a pun. I'd call it a pretty pathetic attempt at humor, myself."

Pause. Clement narrows his eyes and cocks his head.

"Would you indeed?" he growls. "But then, even with something as unimportant as a joke, you must be better than everyone else. Isn't that right, Pagan?"

Oh, get off my back. "When it comes to jokes, Master Clement, I *am* better than everyone else."

"Odd that I've never noticed it."

"You've never noticed it because you don't have a sense of humor."

"Really?"

"Yes, really. And I can prove it with a syllogism. Because all people with a sense of humor laugh, and you don't laugh; therefore you don't have a sense of humor."

He's staring at me like a lizard, his eyes black and unblinking. After a while he says, "We are not studying syllogisms today. We are studying *elocutio*."

Which means that you can't think of a response. Ha! Got you there, didn't I? Think you're so smart, you dried-up old relic. You can't get the better of me. I'll always be one step ahead of you because I'm younger and smarter, and I'm not scared of your ranting no matter how loudly you shout, Master Needle-Nose.

"Nescierunt, neque intellexerunt, in tenebris ambulant."

Here we go again. "'They know not, neither will they understand; they walk in darkness.'"

"And what can you find in that sentence?"

What can I find? A moral reflection? No, if it were a moral reflection, there'd be something about good or evil in it. So it's not *sententia* . . .

"I'm waiting, Pagan."

Then why don't you just wait, instead of flapping your tongue around? Oh—wait—I've got it!

"*Translatio!*"

"Which is?"

"A metaphor."

"And what else?"

What else? What do you mean, what else?

He parts his lips in a savage, toothless grin. "What else can you find in that sentence?" he inquires, and I can't believe he's serious. Something else? There can't be something else!

Frantically thinking, as he spits words at me like arrowheads.

"So, Pagan, perhaps you're not so clever after all. Could it be that the fount of wisdom is beginning to dry up? Don't tell me there's something you don't know. Where is that brilliant mind you're so proud of?"

Shut up! Just shut up!

"Come on, boy, I thought you were an orator. Call yourself a rhetorician? You couldn't talk your way out of bed—"

"Interpretatio!" (You maggot!) *"*The repetition of the same idea in different words!*"*

Dead silence. Even Bernard's stopped reading. And I'm panting as if I've just run a race—panting for breath—and Clement leans forward until we're nose to nose.

"What else?" he hisses.

Blank. Total blank. Turning to look at the others, but they're no help; they just sit there staring, white-faced, and I have to think—I have to figure this out. . . .

"Well?"

Significatio? No. *Membrum?* Can't be.

"Well, Pagan?" His eyes are slits. His voice is a goad. "Could it be that you're stumped? Could it be that you don't know the answer? Of course you don't. Because you're a puffed-up little bantam cock under the mistaken impression that you're an eagle. You're nothing. Compared to the Masters of the Trivium, you're just a worm in a hole. Why don't you admit it? Lost your tongue, now?"

Can't breathe. Can't breathe properly.

"Come on, Pagan, spit it out! Tell me the answer! Surely you know the answer."

"No."

It emerges as a strangled squawk, because the muscles in my throat seem to be paralyzed. Clement puts his hand to his ear.

"What? What was that?"

"No." You stinking scumbag. "I don't know."

"You don't know." He sits back, with a vicious look of satisfaction. "Then I'll tell you, shall I? Shall I tell you, Pagan?"

"Yes! Yes, yes, just tell me!"

"The answer is nothing."

What? I don't understand. Staring into his glittering eyes as he elaborates, softly.

"There is nothing else to be found in that sentence." He's grinning like a skull, like a devil. Triumphantly. "Fooled you there, didn't I? Eh?"

You bastard. You—you—I'm going to kill you. I'm going to *kill you!*

"Pagan—"

Wrench the stick from his hands. Smash it down—*crack!*—on the floor, so hard that it breaks, and one piece goes spinning. But the other piece—I've still got that. Throwing it at him. *"You bastard! You maggot! I hate you, I'm going to kill you!"* He ducks, and it bounces off his arm. Let go! Let go of me! Someone on my back—get off, will you?

Kicking. Writhing. Roland's voice, from somewhere above.

"Pagan, stop! Stop it!"

Get off me! Get *off me*! Scratch—jab—go for
the guts—ouch! You bastard! The knee, the knee!
A sob of pain.

"Stop it!"

Christ! The weight! On the ground, on my
chest, and my arms, I can't—ow! Yeow! Bent back
behind; someone holding me down. Shaking me.
Wrists numb with the pressure.

"That's enough! Stop it!"

Bucking, and he lets go. It worked! No, it didn't.
He's hauling me around. Ow—help—get off! On
my back, face to face . . .

With Roland.

Thwack! He slaps me across the cheek. "Stop it,
Pagan!" *Thwack!* He does it again. "Do you hear
me? You're hysterical! Calm down!"

Can't move. Can't even breathe. Pain in my leg,
my wrist, my head . . . sick in my stomach . . .

What have you done to me, you bastard?

"Pagan? Listen, you have to calm down—"

And I spit in his face.

He reacts as if I've burned him. Rears back,
white as snow; scrambles to his feet; turns away,

gasping. And suddenly a fire is snuffed out in my head. I can see again. I can breathe again. I've got wet checks and sore ribs and—and I'm so tired. . . .

"Pagan?" It's Clement. His voice is very calm. "Pagan, can you hear me?"

"Yes, Master."

"Go and wash your face. Durand, help him up. Take him to wash his face."

"Yes, Master."

And here's Durand. Good old Durand: he's almost as shaky as I am. Why does everyone look so sick? Oh, yes. Yes, I remember, it's my fault. It's my fault because I spat—because I spat—

"Pagan? Listen to me." It's Clement speaking. God, and I broke his walking stick. I'm dead now. I'm finished. "Pagan? I want you to remember something. Will you remember something?"

"Yes, Master."

"Violence is the last refuge of illiterates. It means that you've lost." He taps his forehead. "What we have up here—*up here*—is the deadliest weapon that God has given us. Do you understand?"

"Yes, Master."

"And there's something else." He looks down at the floor, biting his lip. When he looks up again, he's perfectly expressionless. "I intend to order a new staff," he says in the most arid of tones. "I shall inform the cellarer that I broke this staff myself, in an accident. A fall." He glares around the room: at Raymond, at Gaubert, at Durand. His eyes are like embers set deep in his skull. "We will forget," he says coldly, "that this incident ever occurred. It was a mistake. Is that clear?

"It should not have happened."

SPRING 1189

❖

I wish Guilabert would hurry. I want to sit down. Ah! There he is, squeezing through the refectory door, and everyone bows as he waddles his way up the center aisle like a huge milk pudding on legs. Reaches the Abbot's table. Mutters the *Benedicite*. And who's that at the lectern? Not Bernard Blancus! God preserve us, it is Bernard Blancus. This is going to be rough.

"*Edent bauberes,*" he remarks, forcing the words through a noseful of congealed goo, and it's enough to put you off your dinner. He asks us all to pray for him; Guilabert gives the blessing; everyone sits down. Across the table, Bernard catches my eye.

He twirls a lock of hair three times around his index finger.

I know what he's thinking. That's the sign for "Raymond." He's worried that Raymond's going to miss a meal if he doesn't hurry back.

"Bobulus Ziod." (The clogged voice of Bernard Blancus, painfully plowing through the Book of Isaiah.) *"Ecce, Dobidus vediet ad salvadas gedes ed audidab facied . . ."*

And here comes the wine. Oh, no, damn, it's not wine, it's water. I keep forgetting about Lent. Bernard Surdellus pours it very carefully into each cup, as his assistants follow with the bread and beans. So many beans . . . it's going to be fun in the dormitory tonight. All I can say is, someone had better leave the window open.

Splat! The beans. *Splat!* Ladled onto our bread. *Splat!* They're still steaming, but that doesn't deter old Durand. He picks up a mouthful and drops it, instantly, because he's burned himself. Starts blowing on his fingers. Beside him, the new novice swallows a giggle.

I don't like that new novice. What's his name? Gaucher? Always whining. Always complaining. It's too hot, it's too cold, he's hungry, he's tired, his back's sore, he can't eat eggs, he can't sleep properly because Amiel's been coughing all night. Doesn't seem to occur to him that Amiel's the one who should be complaining. And of course he never says a word when Clement's around: just purses his lips and lifts his eyes to the hills whence cometh. Reminds me a bit of the Patriarch of Jerusalem: tall, pale, and slender, just like the Patriach, with the same long neck, the same long eyelashes, and the same petulant personality. Except, of course, that Gaucher's only a boy, so he doesn't have the Patriarch's considerable experience with women.

Watching him as he blows on his beans.

"Cohfordabidi ed iab nolidae dibere; ecce, edib Deus nosder redribued judiciub . . ."

Ugh! That blocked nose! It's as irritating as an unoiled hinge. Ignore it, Pagan, think about something else. Think about . . . God. What *is* there to think about? Certainly not the food. It's never been inspiring at the best of times, and at Lent it's so plain that it's positively Cistercian.

Gaubert nudges me: when I turn, he points at his breastbone (which means *I*), crosses his hands on his chest (*want*), and knocks one forefinger against the other, twice (*eggs*). *I—want—eggs*. Well, so did I, Gaubert, but we won't be getting any.

Ouch! Who did that? Who kicked my ankle? As I look up, Bernard points toward the door. What—? Who—? Oh, I see, it's Raymond.

He's trying to slip in quietly, without causing a disturbance. Hurriedly washing his hands. Bowing in Guilabert's direction. Scurrying across to join us, his face flushed with excitement.

Must have gotten a present from his father.

He stops in front of Clement and begins to make his formal apology (with a great fluttering of fingers), but Clement waves it aside before he's even finished. So he abandons the effort and squeezes in next to me—despite the fact that there's much more room on the opposite bench. Bernard, who's been saving a spot, looks a little put out.

Your—father—well? (Amiel signs from the other end of the table.) *Your—sister—well?*

Raymond nods. He's trying to look calm, but I can feel him quivering. Bernard Surdellus arrives with the food, and there's a pause as Raymond receives his share. I can almost hear the growling of Durand's stomach: he's already finished his beans, and he's casting wistful glances at Raymond's portion. Bernard sticks his thumb in his mouth—it's a sign that means "baby."

Baby? What baby? Oh, that's right; I understand.

Raymond shakes his head, indicating that his
sister still hasn't given birth. He's sitting with his
hands hidden from view, under the tabletop, and
suddenly I can feel him tapping my leg. When I
look at him, he's gazing off toward the lectern.

What the hell is he doing?

Tap-tap. Tap-tap-tap. Reaching down to push his
hand away, but there's something else down
there—a wad of parchment . . .

God save us! It's the letter!

Quickly relieving him of it. Tucking it into my
girdle. Oh, clap your hands, all ye people; shout
unto God with the voice of triumph. I can't believe
it's come. It's actually come! No wonder Raymond's
so excited. No wonder he's sweating like a piece of
cheese. Glancing at him sideways, and he throws
me one of his conspiratorial grins. You gem, Raymond. You bundle of myrrh. I'll never forget this,
never.

But how am I going to read the damned thing?

I'll need time, I'll need light, I'll need privacy—
and I might as well ask for the moon. Tomorrow,
perhaps? When Clement's at chapter? No, that's no

good. *We're* supposed to be going to chapter tomorrow, too, because Raymond's presenting his petition. And of course he'll be accepted. Why wouldn't they want to make him a monk? He's always been the perfect novice, so he's bound to be a perfect monk.

God, how I wish I could read this letter now. I'm so desperate to read it! If only I could just open it up under the table. But I can't, of course—not with all these people watching me. Durand's watching me. Clement's watching me. Roland's watching me. . . .

Roland. He drops his gaze as I look at him, and begins to pick at his bread. Barely a mouthful gone, needless to say. No wonder he's as thin as a whip. No wonder he's so listless. He's going to kill himself—he's going to damn well kill himself, and he can't blame me because it's *all his own fault.* Was it me who stopped talking to him? No. He was the one who stopped talking to *me.* Wouldn't even listen when I tried to apologize that time. That time when I . . . when I . . .

God damn you, Roland! Well you can crawl off under a stone, for all I care, because I'm fed up with your stupid behavior. I don't need you. I don't need that miserable moping; it's driving me insane. I can take care of myself, thank you, and—and—oh, God, I have to stop thinking about this. I have to stop thinking; it hurts too much.

"Rorade, caeli, desuber, ed dubes pluadt jusdub; aberiadur derra ed gerbided salvadoreb . . ."

Sucking the last of the sauce off my fingers. Tearing a piece off my bread. Beside me, Raymond's shoveling his food down like a thief with a stolen capon: you'd think he hadn't eaten in years. I wonder if he's actually read this letter. But I can't just ask him, not in public. I'll have to think of another way.

Nudging him with my foot.

He looks around, chewing, just in time to see me knock his pewter cup to the floor. It hits the tiles with a muffled clang, and Bernard Blancus pauses mid-verse. Apologies, everyone! Apologies, apologies! Giving Raymond another kick, so that he joins me, for a moment, under the table.

Hurry now—can't waste time. Point at him; that means "you." Wag my palm back and forth, like pages turning; that means "read." Make a fist and stamp the air with it, the way you'd stamp a seal; that means "letter." *You—read—letter?* He shakes his head. Curse it! So he can't tell me what's inside.

But before I can climb back onto the bench, he grabs my collar and puts his mouth to my ear. "Tonight," he whispers, and begins to lisp so that the *s* sounds don't carry: "Thtay awake. Bring the letter. I'll take care of it." And he pops back up to his seat like a diver returning to the surface, his empty cup in his hand.

Tonight? What does he mean, "tonight"? Clement glares suspiciously as I slip back into my place. (He doesn't trust me out of his sight for a moment.) Bernard Blancus shuts his book with a bang. Oh, Lord. Is that the end of dinner? I haven't even finished my bread! Stuffing the rest of it into my mouth; scrambling to my feet with the others. Raymond is still madly chewing, and Clement raps the table sharply.

When we look at him, he's looking at Raymond. He waves his right hand, as if to say goodbye, and joins the thumbs and fingers of both hands to make a circle.

Leave—bread.

Poor old Raymond. Didn't even get a decent meal. But I suspect that his father might have fed him: there's a suspicious-looking stain on his wrist that has all the characteristics of honey. Poking him in the ribs as we line up to make our exit. *I— lick?* Pointing at his mysterious, sticky smudge.

He grins. Licks it off himself. Smacks his lips dramatically.

Time for one of our exclusive, private signals. The one involving an extended middle finger.

Up your arse, Raymond.

After you, Pagan.

Smart bastard. I just can't beat him, when it comes to sign language. Still grinning, he tucks his hand into the crook of my arm and leads me out of the refectory.

I wonder what he's planning for tonight.

‡CHAPTER TWENTY-SIX‡

It's a big, bright moon, but not bright enough to read by. So what does Raymond think he's doing? Beckoning to me from the shadows. Scurrying down the path to the herb-garden wall. Has he found himself a candle? A lamp? A torch? Maybe he isn't even going to read the letter. Maybe this is about something else entirely.

Helping him to lift the enormous oak beam.

One of these days, the circator is going to pass this door while I'm still on the other side of it. He's going to pick up the bar and put it back in its slot, and I'm not going to be able to get back in again. I only hope he doesn't do it tonight.

"Quick," Raymond whispers, and opens the door just wide enough for us to squeeze through. He seems very nervous. "The circator's passed, but we mustn't dawdle. He'll be back again soon."

"What's going on?" Softly, into his ear. "What are we supposed to be doing?"

"We're going to the guesthouse."

"The *guesthouse?*"

"Shh! My father is staying there tonight. He's leaving in the morning."

"But—"

"I talked to his squire, Burchard; he's a friend of mine. He promised to give me a lamp."

Ah! I see. Then lead on, Raymond. Following his hunched figure as he turns right and right again, keeping to the beaten earth of the path, moving like a feather past the shuttered windows of our dormitory. It's a beautiful night: a clear, cold, early spring night. Somewhere an owl hoots, and there's a frightened rustle from the pile of dead leaves near the wall.

Mouse, I should think.

Raymond stops at the door of the guesthouse and taps it very softly with his knuckle. Once. Twice. Three times. He's shaking all over, but not from the cold: he's just scared. Something tells me

265

that he doesn't make a habit of wandering around the abbey after dark. Well, he couldn't, could he? Otherwise *I* would have run into him.

Suddenly, a muted noise from inside. The shuffle of footsteps. The creak of a hinge. A hand appears, with a flickering lamp in its palm. When Raymond takes the lamp, the hand is quickly withdrawn, and the door closes.

"I couldn't ask my father," Raymond explains quietly, as we retrace our steps. "My father only agreed to handle this letter because I told him Father Clement knew all about it. He wouldn't approve of what we're doing. He wouldn't understand."

"But Burchard would?"

"Burchard is my friend. Anyway, he's sleeping in the common room. On a table. He's closer to the door."

"But if your father heard you knocking?"

"Burchard will tell him that it was the circator, making his rounds. I've arranged all that."

So I see. And I couldn't have arranged it better myself. "By the way, Raymond, where are we going?" Watching him as he walks along, shielding the fragile flame with his left hand. "I suppose you've worked all that out, too, have you?"

"We're going to the orchard," he replies. "I thought it was the safest place. No one ever goes there at night, and the trees will help to hide us."

"Sounds sensible to me."

"You think so?"

"I don't know of anywhere better."

He smiles, and we press on past the stables, across the bald patches of dry mud and brown grass, not too close to the mill house (where Badilo and the other servants are sleeping), toward the mysterious, moonlit shelter of the orchard. It's so still and peaceful—you'd think we had the whole abbey to ourselves. Nothing but the sound of our footsteps, crunching softly on grass or gravel, padding on carpets of ash or earth. Ahead of us, the dark forest of cherished fruit trees, their new buds wrapped in old rags to protect them from the frost.

If it were autumn there'd be servants stationed all around those trees, to guard the ripening apples. But no one's interested in the orchard right now. It's as safe a place as any.

"Here," says Raymond. "Let's stop here."

"No. We'll go farther in. We've got a light, remember. We want a good screen."

Pushing on through the twisted, clawing boughs,

fending them off carefully, because a single broken twig will show the sharp-eyed gardeners that we've been here. Trying not to leave any footprints. Aha! This is good. This is excellent.

"What about there? Behind that tree trunk?"

"All right." He moves over to it and squats down. "Come on, then, quickly. We don't have all week."

The letter is still where I put it, twisted around my girdle. It has a very ornate seal, with spires and stars and a cross and some Latin words, and I can't help wondering if there's some way of opening the letter without breaking the seal. Seems a pity to spoil such a fine impression. But Raymond won't let me ponder the possibilities; he's on fire with impatience.

"Go on!" he cries. "What does it say? Hurry!"

I've never received a letter before. Never opened one up or read one. It's a wonderful thing, to know that yours are the first and only eyes to alight on a document since it was written and sealed by the person who sent it. The parchment crackles as I smooth it on my leg. The writing is clear and strong, though a little dense in places. Let's see, now. *Eugenius, servus Domini* . . .

"'Eugenius, servant of God, abbot of Voutenay-sur-Cure, greetings and paternal blessings to his beloved son, Brother Raymond of Carcassonne.'"

"That's me," says Raymond, and giggles. "Doesn't it sound good? Brother Raymond . . ."

"You *will* be Brother Raymond, soon."

"Do you think so?"

"Well, of course."

"It's going to be very strange," he murmurs anxiously. "I just hope I can do it."

Oh, come on, Raymond. "After a year of Father Clement? You could do it upside down, with your head in a bag." Turning back to the letter. "'With what grave consternation did I receive your news of Brother Aeldred de Reigny, and how fervently did I pray for guidance in this matter, which has tormented our foundation for many years, though the culprit himself fled these walls long ago.'"

"Bull's-eye!"

"Hold on. 'You suspect a hidden blemish in Brother Aeldred's past. You require a full account of his time here. My son, this man's life is a catalog of heinous acts; he is a slave to the vile and viperine powers of his own depravity. His sins, against which Saint Paul warned us in Romans Chapter

One, Verse Twenty-seven, are manifold and loathsome in every particular.'"

Exchanging looks. Romans Chapter One, Verse Twenty-seven? Raymond remembers it first.

"'And likewise also the men, leaving the natural use of the woman, burned in their lust one toward another,'" he quotes.

"Oh, yes. Of course. 'Men with men working that which is unseemly.'" (How could I ever forget?)

"Keep going. What else does he say?"

"Hmmm. Where was I? 'The corruption of innocents, the impurity of vile affections, the abuse of trust and privilege: all these sins were his, and more, for not least of his abominable offenses was his impenitence, his utter lack of shame, arising from a most terrible and diabolic arrogance of the soul. Oh, what iniquity! Oh, what foul and degenerate perversions! Shun this man, my son; cast him from your midst; cleanse your fraternity as you would cleanse yourself from all filthiness of the flesh and spirit, perfecting holiness in the fear of God, and in the name of the Holy and Undivided Trinity.'"

Sweet saints preserve us. He certainly feels strongly about it. Look up at Raymond, who's sitting there with his mouth open.

"I'm beginning to wonder if we've got the right Aeldred." (Voicing the worry that's been lurking at the back of my mind.) "This is all a bit hysterical, don't you think? Did you describe him the way I told you to?"

"Of course I did!" (He's offended now.) "Red hair, pale blue eyes, snub nose, narrow shoulders . . ."

"Then it must be him. How amazing. The way this abbot talks, it makes Aeldred sound like the Beast of the Apocalypse."

"Perhaps he is. Underneath."

"Perhaps." Returning to the letter. "'My son, if you think me intemperate in my language, let me say that I use only those words that will spur you to action. I believe that my former restraint in speaking of this matter may have inspired your brethren with doubts, and caused them to temper their judgment with mercy, where none was deserved.'"

"Mercy?" Raymond interrupts. "What's he talking about? What 'former restraint'?"

"I don't know. Shh! Let me finish. 'For I was grieved to learn that this canker, this serpent, still lived among you, and that my warnings had gone unheeded. Where is Brother Montazin de

Castronovo? Why has he not conveyed to you that which I told him, last spring, in reply to his urgent entreaties regarding the same, notorious malefactor? My son, the infection of Aeldred de Reigny's impious lust has gone unchastened for too long. It *must* be cauterized. Take heed, and in fearful contemplation of future judgment, protect with unshakeable strength the sanctity of your house from the defilement of a man condemned to the eternal flames of hell.'"

Glory. Oh, glory. This is it. This is *it!*

"I don't understand," Raymond objects. "Is he saying that Father Montazin already knew about Aeldred?"

"Well, of course he did!" And suddenly it hits me. "I never told you that, did I? I never told you about Montazin."

"No." Deep in Raymond's shadowy eyes, the reflection of a single flame leaps and flickers. "So you'd better tell me now, hadn't you?"

"Montazin knows everything. He's blackmailing Aeldred, just as Centule is. He's making him take stolen money to a woman called Beatrice, because she's his cousin. Montazin's cousin, I mean, not Aeldred's cousin." Pausing a moment, so that

Raymond has time to absorb it all. His lamp-lit face looks blank with shock. "You see, when Montazin found out that I knew what he was doing, he played that trick with the girl. So I'd be completely discredited."

"But I thought Roquefire—?"

"Roquefire is working with Montazin. So is Sicard the guest-master. That's one reason why I couldn't have sent a letter myself. Sicard handles all the monastery letters, and if he'd seen something addressed to the Abbot of Voutenay-sur-Cure . . . well, you can imagine what would have happened."

Slowly, Raymond shakes his head. When he speaks, he sounds breathless. Awestruck.

"You found this out by yourself?" he whispers. "All on your own?"

"I had to."

"But—but what will you do now?"

"Now? Now I have *proof!* I have proof, Raymond! Written proof!" Waving the letter at him. "And I'm going to show it to the Abbot, as soon as he returns."

"He's not returning until next week."

"I can wait."

"But why don't you show it to Father Guilabert?"

"Because I don't trust Guilabert. I don't trust any of them. Only the Abbot." Folding up my precious letter. Tucking it carefully into my girdle. "I won't be parted from this until I can put it straight into his hands."

Raymond seems to be thinking. His hair shines like gold in the lamplight. His skin looks very pale. "If you wait until the Abbot comes back," he says, "I may not be a novice anymore when you tell him."

"So?"

"So you won't forget about me, will you? You'll tell me what happens?"

"Well, of course I will!" God, Raymond. "How could I possibly forget about you?"

Silence falls. I'm beginning to get a bit cold, sitting here under the trees. On the damp earth. Without my cowl or scapular.

Maybe it's time to go in.

"We should probably move now, Raymond. We're running out of time." Scrambling to my feet; dusting off my robe.

But his hand shoots up and drags me back down again.

"Wait," he says. "Wait, I—I just want to ask you something. . . ."

Pause. Well, come on. What is it?

"Ask me what?"

"About women." He swallows. "Have you—have you ever—actually—you know . . ."

"Bedded one?"

"Yes." Even in this light, I can see the blush. "Have you ever done that?"

Oh, Lord. Here we go. "Yes."

"You have?"

"Yes."

"A lot?"

"No."

"How many times?"

"Jesus, Raymond, I don't know." What a question! "Twice? No, three times."

"What . . ." He hesitates. "What was it like?"

What was it like? I'll tell you what it was like. It was like hell, the first time. Back in Jerusalem, when I was fourteen, and that girl and her friends . . . But I won't think about that. Anyway, the second time was better. Last year, on the ship to Marseille, when Roland was seasick and I met that widow. Marguesia the widow. She was nice. Old, but nice. I wonder what happened to her.

"It's all right, I suppose." Thinking about the last time, with Marguesia. But I'd better not dwell on it.

If I do, I'll just get hot and bothered. "Actually, it can be a lot of fun."

Raymond sighs.

"There are so many things I haven't done," he murmurs. "And if I become a monk tomorrow . . . well, I'll never do them, will I? Not ever."

Uh-oh. "What's the matter, Raymond? Don't you want to be a monk?"

"I suppose I do. It's just—I don't know." He stares down at the lamp. "I just wish I was more like you, that's all. I wish I'd done everything."

Done everything? What's that supposed to mean?

"Raymond, I haven't done much, you know. I've wasted half my life messing around."

"But you've *done* things!" he cries, and startles himself so much that he quickly covers his mouth. We sit for a moment, listening.

Nothing stirs.

"I'm going to miss you," he finally remarks. "I never thought I would, but I will. It's a shame that—well—you know."

"Yes, I know." It's a shame that we didn't work this out earlier. Watching him as he prods the ground with a stick, a scowl on his face, a dead leaf entangled in his hair. He looks very young for his

276

age, like all the former oblates: very young, but also, in a peculiar fashion, very old. I don't know what it is. Something to do with the lack of worldly experience, combined with the dead weight of long hours in church.

Poor sod. Poor miserable sod. He doesn't belong here, in this desolate graveyard of a monastery; he should be out managing estates, with his father.

"I'll miss you, too, Raymond." Carefully avoiding his eye. "It's just not going to be the same without you."

And we make our way slowly back to the guest-house.

CHAPTER TWENTY-SEVEN

Here comes Raymond. He looks pale but composed. The church is so quiet that every one of his footsteps echoes around the vaults like the crack of a whip. He's carrying his Act of Profession in both hands, reverently, the way you'd carry a fragment of the True Cross.

He stops in front of the altar, where Montazin is waiting for him.

Poor Raymond. I can see him shrinking back as Montazin reaches for the roll of parchment. How awful to have that tapeworm reading out your Act of Profession, when you know exactly what he's been doing. The sonorous voice booms away ("... *stabilitas loci* ... *conversio morum* ..."), while the monks yawn and fidget, and the novices nudge each other, and Bernard Incentor wipes his eyes.

I feel so sorry for Bernard. He and Raymond haven't been apart since they were six days old; they even shared the same wet nurse, Raymond tells me. But now Clement says that Bernard isn't ready to become a monk. So the two friends are separated, and it seems pointlessly cruel, even though it's just what you'd expect from a heartless brute like Clement. God, how I hate that man sometimes.

"Dominus det vobis societatem electorum suorum." Montazin finishes reading the Act, solemnly lays it on the altar, and withdraws at a stately pace, his chiseled nose in the air. Anyone would think that he was swearing in a monarch. But I don't mind watching him swank about anymore, because I know that his days among the Elect are well and truly numbered. Enjoy it while you can, pushead. You're heading for the biggest fall since Lucifer's.

"Suscipe me secundum . . ." Raymond prostrates himself and tries to recite the versicle. But the poor thing is so nervous that his voice comes out as a strangled squawk. So he clears his throat and starts again.

"Suscipe me secundum eloquium tuum, Domine, et vivam, et ne confundas me ab exspectatione mea . . ."

Hah! And there's Guilabert, all dressed up in the Abbot's cope. Holding the Abbot's pastoral staff in his pudgy hand. As if he could ever stand in for the Abbot! God, if only the Abbot were here. How am I ever going to wait until Tuesday? It's such a strain, walking around with this letter tucked into my drawers. I'm so scared I'm going to lose it before I have a chance to show it to him.

"Suscipe me secundum eloquium tuum . . ." Raymond prostrates himself for the second time and repeats the versicle. He's getting more confident now.

I wonder how he'll cope as a fully fledged monk. It'll be awful, sleeping in the same dormitory as Montazin. And Sicard. And Aeldred, too! God, imagine sharing a room with Aeldred! Enough to make your flesh crawl. I know *I* couldn't do it.

"Suscipe me secundum eloquium tuum . . ." Raymond's voice, high-pitched and breathless. Down he goes, flat on the floor again, racing through his third recitation as if he's trying to win a prize. When he finishes, he scrambles to his feet, and Guilabert also rises, hoisting his bulk off the Abbot's throne with little grunts, like a pig. He comes forward

until he's standing beside Raymond. Clears his throat. Raises his staff.

"*Kyrie eleison,*" he bleats, and everyone makes the standard response: "*Kyrie eleison.*"

"*Christe eleison.*"

"*Christe eleison.*"

"*Pater noster, qui es in caelis, sanctificetur nomen tuum.*"

Only Guilabert could make the "Our Father" sound like a list of farriers' supplies. He's even mispronouncing the Latin. Glancing at Clement, who looks as if he's just bitten into a sour grape. (Nobody hates a bungled inflection as much as Clement.) He catches me staring at him and rolls his eyes—something I've never seen him do before. It's almost as if he's trying to say: "Listen to that hopeless bungler."

How very odd.

"*Et ne nos inducas in tentationem sed libera nos a malo, amen,*" Guilabert intones, and now it's time for Psalm Fifty-one. The terrible, the unbearable *Miserere.*

Have mercy on me, O God, according to Thy goodness, according to the multitude of Thy tender mercies wipe out my transgressions.

"*Miserere mei, Deus, secundum misericordiam tuam*

281

secundum multitudinem miserationum tuarum dele iniquitatem meam . . ."

As the deep, gentle chorus rises slowly, like incense, toward the golden stars on the ceiling, Bernard Blancus comes forward with Raymond's new cowl. Guilabert blesses it, and with his head bowed beneath the pure strains of the psalm, he manages to achieve a certain degree of dignity.

"Tibi soli peccavi et quod malum est coram te feci."

Turning, he places the cowl on Raymond's head and kisses him on both cheeks. Once. Twice. Three times. The chorus swells and fades, and a shower of silvery notes seems to enfold Raymond like a shaft of light, as all at once the music and the images merge into one glorious, inexpressible sensation: the glitter of the altar screen, the soaring voices, the smell of incense, the graceful and pious embrace, the loving smile of the Holy Virgin, painted in rainbow colors above the choir, as she bends down from her heavenly throne with her hand raised in blessing.

God. Oh, God. It's so beautiful.

"Ut manifesteris iustis in sententia tua, rectus in ludicio tuo . . ."

Let Thy majesty be justified in Thy sentence, vindicated when Thou wouldst condemn.

Slowly, one by one, the monks leave their places, approach the altar, and give Raymond the kiss of peace. They move so smoothly, identical in their long black robes, that it almost looks like a dance—or like the majestic movement of stars across the sky. But when it's Clement's turn, he breaks the rhythm, because he can hardly walk now, and he drags himself step by step across the floor of the church, his walking stick rapping against the tiles, until he reaches Raymond in front of the altar. Transferring the stick to his left hand, he leans forward to kiss Raymond's cheek—and suddenly they're hugging each other, very tight, and it feels as if a steel splinter has pierced me right through the heart.

Because I know: suddenly I know. I know that I'm never going to be up there in front of that altar, receiving the kiss of peace. I'm never going to present my Act of Profession. I'm never going to do it because I—because—

Because I'm never going to be a monk.

It's so clear to me now. They'll never let me in, no matter how hard I try. And why should they? I don't belong here. I can't even imagine myself as one of these men, shuffling around and around the same solemn path, day after day, year after year, with nothing to sustain me but my love of God, which I have to admit is in a pretty sad state at the moment. Not at all the flourishing, healthy faith that it should be. In fact I can't help wondering if He actually knows what's going on down here sometimes. I can't help thinking that people like me—well, that we're too insignificant to attract His attention.

"Ecce in culpa natus sum et in peccato concepit me mater mea."

Behold, I was shaped in wickedness, and in sin hath my mother conceived me.

It's the story of my life, that verse. Shaped in wickedness, conceived in sin. I'll never make it at Saint Martin's; I've known that, deep in my gut, ever since I joined. Nothing's been holding me here except the prospect of avenging myself. But when Montazin is disgraced, what shall I do then? Where shall I go? There's nothing out there, absolutely nothing. And if Roland stays . . . if Roland . . .

Roland. Oh, God. He's the reason I came here in the first place, and now—Christ, I can't bear it. Where is he? He's gone. He's just not there anymore, not for me. Not for anyone. He's an empty shell, and even the shell looks different. Hollow-eyed. Stooping. Wasted. Like a candle that's been snuffed out. Like a walking corpse. I can't—oh, God, oh, God, I've lost him, I've lost Roland, and I can't stand it. I can't stand it anymore. Oh, God, why are you doing this? Why are you doing this to me? I can't even sing, or I'll choke on my own tears. Trying to hide them. Trying to stop them, with one hand over my mouth, but the psalm goes on and on, so anguished and poignant and heart-rending, and it's going to kill me, I just know it is. Cast me not away from Thy presence, and take not Thy holy spirit from me. Restore unto me the joy of Thy salvation, and uphold me with Thy free spirit.

A hand slips into mine.

It's Durand, of course: he squeezes hard. I can't see his face, through the tears, but I know what he's doing. Staring at me. Peering at me. Why doesn't he leave me alone? When I try to pull my hand away, he holds on tight and starts to stroke it. Don't do that, God, please, don't do that! You're only making it worse.

The sacrifices of God are a troubled spirit, a broken and contrite heart; O God, shalt Thou not despise.

And the psalm goes on. Phrase by agonizing phrase. Winding its way to the end of the office, as it slowly tears me to pieces.

‡CHAPTER TWENTY-EIGHT‡

The Abbot's back today, hooray, hooray, hooray.

The Abbot's back today, hooray, hooray, hooray.

Hell on earth, it's that stupid song again. I can't get the damned thing out of my head. And I must have been dreaming it, too, because it's been knocking around my skull ever since I woke up. For God's sake, Pagan, think about something else! Think about what you're doing, here. You're supposed to be reciting the litany, not some inane, tuneless nursery rhyme. I know you're still half asleep, but you've got to pull yourself together.

"*Kyrie eleison.*"

"*Kyrie eleison.*"

"*Christe eleison.*"

"Christe eleison."

And there's Guilabert, wobbling across the floor. How wonderful to think that this is going to be his last Lord's Prayer for at least two weeks. Two weeks! Just think, we'll have the Abbot leading the offices tonight. The Abbot, with his intelligent face. And his trim figure. And his clear, precise, mellifluous Latin.

The Abbot's back today, hooray, hooray, hooray.

I wonder when he'll be arriving. Not quite yet, I suppose. He certainly won't be here until sunrise. Probably not until this afternoon. They said Tuesday afternoon. God, I wish he'd hurry! I simply *have* to get rid of this letter.

"Pater noster," Guilabert drones, *"qui in caelis, sanctificetur nomen tuum . . ."*

And then, of course, there's the question of how I'm actually going to do it. How the hell does a nobody like me secure a private audience with Anselm? I'd have an easier time securing a seat beside the Lord God Almighty on Judgment Day. My only hope is that Anselm never fails to visit the novices when he comes back from his trips. Perhaps I'll ask if I can speak to him then. Immediately. On a matter of the most crucial importance.

Regarding a certain Montazin.

"*Et ne nos inducas in tentationem sed libera nos a malo,*" Guilabert concludes, and everyone says, "Amen." At last! It's over! There's an air of subdued restlessness as the monks slowly file out the southern door: they all want to get to the cloisters quickly and wash their faces while the water's still hot. Personally, I don't think I've washed my face in hot water since I arrived here. But then, I'm just a humble novice.

A nudge in the ribs. It's Bernard. He curls a strand of hair around his finger and briefly covers his eyes with his left hand. *Raymond—absent.* Really? Raymond's absent? I didn't even notice. Standing on tiptoe to peer over the milling heads, but it's impossible to see everyone in this light. With all those cowls pulled over their faces. I wouldn't know if Raymond was here or not— especially since he worships with the monks now. It's been hard to keep track of him since he became a monk.

Another barrage of signs from Bernard. *Raymond—sick?* Well, don't ask me, Bernard. How should I know? I haven't spoken to Raymond since he presented his Act of Profession. Neither has anyone else, in fact. Isn't he supposed to be keeping silent for three days?

Making a fist, with the thumb turned down. *I know not.*

Bernard frowns and begins to gnaw at his fingernails. Clement pushes me into line.

And out we march, into the cloisters.

Hello, hello. What's happening here? A cluster of notables, all deep in conversation. The prior. The chamberlain. The cellarer. The sacristan. Muttering away by the chapter-house door, shadowy and suspicious in the flickering torch light. How disgraceful. They shouldn't be talking like that. It's supposed to be a silent time. As Clement emerges, they all turn, and Rainier beckons to him.

Surely the Abbot can't have arrived yet?

Wash, Clement tells us, with an imperious gesture. *Wash—and—wait.* He hobbles off to join the conspirators, leaving us to splash around in the bowl of tepid water that's been left on a stool near the book presses. There are three towels set out beside it, all of them sopping. So we end up drying ourselves on our sleeves, as usual.

Abbot—come? Durand inquires after he wipes his face. He's not asking anyone in particular: he's just asking. Some of the monks, I notice, are asking the same question. They're supposed to be pacing around the cloisters in silent contemplation, but most of them are watching the group by the chapter house. I wonder what could possibly be going on over there.

Suddenly Clement breaks away from the group. He limps across the cloister garth toward us, looking particularly formidable, and you can't help thinking that he's about to bite someone's head off. (Please, God, don't let it be mine.) When he reaches us, however, he just stands for a moment, lost in thought.

And when he speaks, his voice is so low that it's almost a whisper.

"We can't use the chapter house for recitations this morning," he says quickly. "It will be needed for an emergency council. Go back to the dormitory, and wait for me there. If I haven't returned by the time the bell rings for Matins, go to the church without me. Roland, you can lead the recitations."

"But Master—" Gaubert begins.

"Shh!" Clement draws his finger across his mouth. "No talking! Just go!"

Emergency council? What could that be for? Trailing after Roland, who leads the way across the cloister garth, through the covered passage, into the herb garden. Moving on feather-light feet past the oblates' dormitory, because they'll be in bed (lucky bastards). Filing back into our own room, where it still smells of night farts.

Black as the Bottomless Pit, as well, because Clement always snuffs the candle out when we leave for Nocturnes.

"I can't see a thing!" Bernard hisses. "They should have given us a lamp."

"Shh!" It's Amiel's voice—a mouse's squeak in the darkness. "You'll wake the oblates."

"Yes, that's right." (Durand.) "We *will* wake the oblates. How are we going to do recitations without waking the oblates?"

"Maybe we shouldn't do recitations," Bernard whispers. But Roland won't have that.

"Father Clement told us to recite," he says in the flat and lifeless voice that he's been adopting lately. It makes you want to punch him in the guts, just to get some kind of human response out of him. "If you speak softly, Bernard, you won't wake the oblates. Now why don't you start the recitations for us?"

"Why don't *you* start?" Bernard retorts, and continues urgently: "Did anyone see Raymond this morning? I didn't see him, did you?"

"Bernard, please, Father Clement—"

"Oh, shut up, Roland! I'm asking a question, here. Did anyone see him?"

"No."

"No."

"Maybe he's sick," Amiel suggests.

"Or maybe his father's here?" Gaubert sounds uncertain. "Maybe that's why there was that fuss in the cloisters."

"Because of a guest? Don't be a fool."

"Bernard, please. There's no call for that."

"Up your arse, Roland! I'm worried about him! He should have been there!"

Knock-knock-knock! A rap on the door. Someone moves (I can hear his knees cracking), and by some miraculous stroke of luck, he finds the door handle. There's a creak of hinges, and all at once the room is flooded with light.

A servant stands on the threshold with a lamp in his hand.

"Is Pagan there?" he asks. It's Badilo, from the mill. "Pagan? Are you there?"

"Yes." (What's this about?) "I'm here."

"Father Clement wants to see you, Pagan. In the guesthouse."

"The guesthouse?"

"Right away."

What could Clement be doing in the guest-house?

"There!" Gaubert says. "I told you that Raymond's father must have come."

But I can't catch Bernard's reply, because I'm out the door already. Trying to keep up with Badilo.

Anyone would think he was running for his life.

"Oi! Badilo! Wait for me!"

He doesn't even stop; he just disappears into the refectory, tossing a gruff remark over his shoulder. "I'm busy, Pagan, you know where the guest-house is."

Busy? At this time of night? What's he doing, masturbating? Trying to perfect the art of snoring through one nostril? This is ridiculous.

Passing into the cloisters, and they're deserted. Completely empty. Where is everyone? In the chapter house? In the guesthouse? Reaching the guesthouse door—the inner door—and pushing it open. Inside, the common room is dark and silent. But there's a faint glow coming from some-where down the passage to my left.

Aha. I see. Someone's in the end room: there's light spilling over the threshold. Should I announce my presence, or will I get my knuckles rapped for not using sign language? Moving forward, past the shuttered windows on my right, past the black, yawning doorways opposite them. Hello? Is that you, Master Needle-Nose?

Whump!

On my knees. On the floor. What—? Who—? Someone hit me . . .

"Where's the letter?"

That's Montazin's voice. Augh! Help! Weight on my back. Grip on my collar. Choking . . .

"Give it to me! Give me the letter, or I'll kill you!"

The voice is right next to my ear. Quick! Now! Throw my head back. *Thunk!* Bone on bone. Got him! He yelps and loosens his grip. Jabbing with the elbow; hitting something soft. Roll with the weight, Pagan, roll with the weight! Pulling him over, kicking his legs, and he rolls along with me. Onto his back. Tries to keep me pinned, but if I drive my toes into his knee—there! He lets go, howling, and I roll off him, onto my stomach.

Quick, quick! Get away! "Help! *Help me—oof!"* Ow! God, my arm, my arm! What's he got? Jesus Christ, it's a candlestick! A great, big, bronze— ow! Help! Stop it! Help!

"Where is it?" (*Thunk!*) "Give it to me!" (*Thunk!*) Ow! Christ! What's he doing? Try to get up. Try to

294

get away. I've got to get away, or he'll kill me. He's going to kill me. My legs won't work. God, my mouth. I can't see. . . .

Blood.

"Where is it?" His weight again. Fumbling hands. He's pulling at my scapular, and the pain— Jesus, the pain—and he's reaching under my robe, and it's the letter—he's looking for the letter—

Punch at his face, but I didn't—oh, help—

Whump!

Flash of light. Stars. The taste in my mouth, and he's still there. Don't hit me, please—Jesus, don't hit me—

"Pagan!"

Roland? Is that you? Suddenly, an impact; weight hitting weight. Cries. Blows. Feet everywhere. Look up (I'm so dizzy) and it's Roland. It is Roland. Praise God, he's here, and he's punching him and punching him and driving his head into the wall, again and again, and he's shouting and screaming. Take that, Montazin, you bastard, I hope he kills you. Oh, Christ. Oh, Christ, I feel so ill.

"Roland!" It's Clement. "Roland, stop! Roland!" There he is, and he sounds so scared.

It's all very muddled. . . . I can't see. . . . What's he doing? He's grabbing Roland's arm, but Roland ignores him. Roland's got the candlestick now. He's pounding it into Montazin's head.

"Roland!" Clement screams, and raises his stick, and brings it down on Roland's spine. It's not a heavy blow, but it does the job. Roland staggers. He turns. He drops the candlestick and he drops Montazin.

Montazin slides to the floor.

"Pagan." Roland's voice is so low that I can hardly hear it, even though he's beside me now. Even though he's kneeling, and I can feel his hands on my face, on my chest, on my shoulders. Holding my head. "Oh, Pagan. Oh, God, God, Pagan, God . . ." He sounds as if he's in pain, terrible pain, but *I'm* the one who's bleeding.

"The letter." Did I speak? I can't even tell. "The letter—take the letter." It's in my drawers. I have to get it. I have to give it to him. Move my hand—

Jesus Christ!

Flash.

Pain.

Darkness.

CHAPTER TWENTY-NINE

"The letter. The letter . . ."

"It's all right, Pagan, I have the letter. I gave it to the Abbot. Do you hear me? It's all right."

The Abbot. The Abbot? You mean he's here? Open my eyes, but everything's blurred. No, wait, it's clearing. And my head—God! My head's going to split. My mouth is so sore.

Roland.

His face, hanging over me: drawn, pale, heavy-eyed. His long nose, and his scar, and the fuzz of gold on his unshaven cheek. Oh, Roland. Oh, Roland.

"The Abbot has read your letter," he says. "You mustn't worry. Everything is going to be all right."

"You're here."

"Yes, I'm here."

"He wath going to kill me!"

"Shh. You're safe, now. I won't leave you."

"Roland." What's the matter with my mouth? I can't move it. I can't speak properly. "My mouth—"

"It's swollen. You've lost a tooth."

"And my arm—"

"Your wrist is broken. Your head is injured. Don't talk, Pagan. You have to rest."

His voice sounds odd. No, it's not his voice; it's my ear. There's something in my ear. "Ith there blood in my ear?"

"Blood?"

"It'th not working. My ear . . ." Reaching up to touch it. Ouch! Shooting pain. Heavy splint.

"Don't move that arm, Pagan."

"My ear—"

"Leave it. It's probably the bandages."

"My head hurth." And my ribs ache. And my mouth is burning and my back is sore and I can't even hear properly.

But at least I'm alive.

Looking up at him. At Roland. He's holding my hand—my good hand—and his fingers are warm. Nice and warm.

"You came." You came, and you saved my life. "How did you know? Why did you come?"

"Father Clement returned just after you left. He asked us where you were."

Roland closes his eyes for a moment. Suddenly he looks old: very, very old.

"When I heard him say that, I—I knew," he murmurs. "Somehow I knew. I knew that something was wrong, and I ran to the guesthouse." A pause. "Clement must have followed me. I don't know. I don't remember. All I remember is you, on the ground . . ." He closes his eyes again, tightly. He bows his head and lifts my hand and presses it to his brow. "I thought you were dead," he gasps. "You were lying there all covered in blood, and he was hitting you, and for an instant—just for one instant—but it seemed like forever. And it was all my fault. All of it."

What? What are you talking about? "My lord—"

"Forgive me, Pagan." He's leaning on the bed, on his elbows, with my hand still pressed to his forehead and his eyes firmly shut. He sounds as if he's choking. "You must forgive me, please. I was going mad. It was the pain, you see, I—it was the pain. The pain of losing Esclaramonde. I thought it would get better, but it only got worse. Worse and worse until everything was dark, all the time. I couldn't breathe. I couldn't sleep. Sometimes I felt as if I were in a little box, a dark little box, and it was getting smaller and smaller. I thought it was God's punishment, and I was ashamed—so ashamed of loving a heretic."

Oh, Jesus. "My lord—"

"And then one day I remembered something. Something that you told me, once, about following my own path. And it suddenly made sense. Because there's a chapter in the Rule of Saint Benedict that says: 'Set nothing whatsoever before Christ.' And in the gospels, too—in the gospels Christ tells us: 'He that loveth father or mother more than me is not worthy of me, and he that loveth son or daughter more than me is not worthy of me.' And I saw that it must be true, because if you love a person, and that person dies . . ." He pauses, overcome.

"Roland—"

"But God will never die," he continues quickly, opening his eyes and raising his head. "God will never die, or be hurt, and so there won't be any pain, you see. No pain at all. If you can only break the bonds that hold you to the earth, and dedicate your heart to God, then you'll be more than a perfect monk. You'll be at peace. In the light. With no one to hurt you anymore."

And you tried that, didn't you? That's what you've been trying to do. You've been trying to wall yourself in.

"But I wasn't thinking of you," he groans. "I was thinking of myself. And you turned away, and were in danger, and I didn't know—I didn't know what you were doing. If I'd known—if I'd cared—I could have protected you. This would never have happened. It never occurred to me that *you* would be hurt."

In more ways than one, Roland. But I can't say it. My mouth is too sore.

"I knew it when I saw you there on the ground," he says wearily. "I knew then that it was all wrong. Or perhaps it's right—I don't know—but I can't do it. I can't be a good monk. I can't dedicate my whole heart to God, because I care about you too much. You and my mother and Esclaramonde. All of you. They're both dead now, but you're still alive. How can I stand by, and see you hurt, and not suffer? I can't. It's impossible, even if you hate me. So it looks as if I'll just have to suffer."

301

God, Roland. Hate you? How can you say that? "I don't hate you. I wath angry, that time. I wath hurt. I didn't mean it . . ."

"Now, now. No talking." It's Elias. Elias? Oh, of course, I must be in the infirmary. I should have recognized those herbs hanging from the rafters.

Elias's face, with its bloodshot eyes. He's carrying a cup.

"Now that you're awake," he says, "you can drink this. It will help with the pain." He lifts my head, rests the cup on my bottom lip. Ow! Ouch! "Come along, drink up."

Yuck! Ugh! That's revolting!

"Just a bit more . . . that's it . . . there. And now you can have a spoonful of honey, to take the taste away."

No, please, just leave me alone.

"I don't think he wants any honey, Father." Roland's anxious voice. "Perhaps his mouth is too sore."

"Very well. No honey." Elias touches my cheek, my wrist, my shoulder. He gives me a pat. "Now don't you move, whatever you do. If you need anything, just call me. I'll be over with Montazin."

Montazin? Where? Where's Montazin? Trying

302

to turn my head as he walks away, but I can't—it's like a knife through my skull. God! Help!

"Montathin . . ."

"It's all right, he won't hurt you." Roland takes my hand again. "He's in bed. He—I—he's not—he can't hurt you, Pagan."

"I thought you killed him."

"No." A pause. "Not quite."

Not quite, but almost. Montazin. Wait a moment. Montazin!

"How did he find out? How did he find out about the letter?"

"Pagan, you shouldn't talk—"

"But *how?*"

"We found another letter, beneath his pillow," Roland speaks with great reluctance. "It must have arrived yesterday. It was from the same man who wrote your letter, the Abbot of Voutenay-sur-Cure. He was asking about the letter that Raymond sent, and why Montazin hadn't informed the community about Aeldred's sins."

So that's it. Of course. I should have considered—I should have realized—

"But I didn't put my name to that letter. Raymond did. How could Montathin—?" Raymond. God.

Raymond. Staring at Roland, and he's avoiding my eye. He's looking down at the blankets. "Where ith he?"

"Pagan—"

"*Where ith he?*"

"Nobody knew. He was missing when the monks rose for Nocturnes." Roland's tone is one I'd almost forgotten: his Commander-of-the-Temple tone. Dry. Clear. Expressionless. "We couldn't ask Montazin, because he's been unconscious all day. Then, after Prime, a girl came. A girl from the village." Throwing me a sideways glance. "It was the same girl."

"Thaurimunda . . ."

"She said she was in the compound last night. Waiting."

"For Roquefire?" I don't believe it. But Roland shakes his head.

"For you, Pagan. She was waiting for you."

"For *me*? But I never had anything to do with her!" (This is insane!) "I haven't laid eyeth on her thince Roquefire put her in our dormitory—"

"I know that, Pagan." Soothingly. "She didn't say that you had *arranged* to meet her. She was just waiting. In case you happened to appear."

"But why?" I don't understand.

Roland's face is like a mask: he seems to be counting my fingers, one by one. Finally he looks up and says: "She seems to regard you with a great deal of affection."

Oh, Lord. You don't mean—you can't mean—

"It was a full moon," Roland continues. "She was waiting near the kitchens when she saw a young monk emerge from the herb garden. She says that she knew he was young because of the way he walked; he was wearing a cowl, so she couldn't see his face. But she thought that he might be you. So she followed him." Pause. "She didn't say anything. She just wanted to see you. To look at your face."

Sweet saints preserve us.

"She followed him through the orchard, to the old well. And she saw that there was another monk there, waiting for him. A tall monk."

"What happened?"

"Father Clement went there this morning and found a little note. It was written in charcoal, on a page torn from a book. It said: 'Meet me at the well tonight,' and it was signed with your name—"

"*What happened, damn you?!*"

He can't tell me. Look, he can't tell me. He's just staring—staring at his hands. Staring at *my* hand.

"He's dead, Pagan." Quietly. "Raymond is dead."

No. Oh, no.

"The girl says that Montazin jumped on him. Threatened him with a knife and demanded the letter. Raymond told him that you had it. Then Montazin must have panicked. He asked if anyone else knew about the letter and Raymond said no, so Montazin stabbed him—"

"No."

"—and threw him down the well. He threw the knife down there, too. He left the note, so that you would be blamed if anyone found the body. (I don't know how he was going to explain the blood on his clothes.) But it would only work if he took the letter from you, and he had to move quickly, because he guessed that you would be showing it to the Abbot, who was returning today. So when the alarm went out for Raymond, he asked Guilabert to call an emergency chapter: that way Clement would have to leave us by ourselves. Then Montazin slipped away and told Badilo to tell you that Clement wanted you in the guesthouse—Pagan? Please, Pagan, don't cry—I can't bear it."

No. Not Raymond. Not Raymond, not him. You can't do this. Please, please don't do this. It can't be true. Oh, God. Oh, God.

"Pagan—Pagan, please—"

"It wath my fault! It wath all my fault!"

"No. *No.*"

"Oh, God . . . oh, God . . ."

"Pagan, listen to me. It wasn't your fault. It was Montazin. Montazin did this. You mustn't blame yourself. Pagan? Pagan, stop it—you'll make yourself ill. Pagan! *Father Elias, come here! Quickly!* Pagan, calm down. Shh. Shh. Oh, please don't, please—I can't bear it . . ."

☩CHAPTER THIRTY☩

How empty the chapter house looks with so many people missing. Aeldred and Montazin. Sicard. Raymond . . .

No. Don't think about Raymond. You mustn't think about Raymond. Think about someone else—think about Aeldred. No! On second thought, I don't want to think about Aeldred, either. It was too awful, the way they dragged him off to the Bishop's Court. The way he cried and groveled and tried to hold on to pieces of furniture. That's something I want to forget.

And Montazin, too; I'd rather forget Montazin. He may have deserved it, but . . . God, it's frightening. It's horrible. Once he was a man, and now he's—what? Half a man? Sitting there blank-eyed, drooling, making vague gestures and uttering meaningless words. I'm glad that they sent him away to the Bishop's Court. I don't want to see him again. I don't want to see what Roland did to him with that candlestick.

One more blow, and Montazin could have done the very same thing to me.

Who else is missing? Sicard, at the Bishop's Court. Rainier, also at the Bishop's Court, but not to stand trial: just to explain what's been going on. So Bernard Blancus is doing Rainier's job, and Bernard Surdellus is doing Sicard's job, and Elias is doing Aeldred's job, and Guilabert is doing Montazin's job, and that's why the food is so awful these days.

Oh! And not to forget Roquefire, of course. Roquefire's gone off to Carcassonne with the rest of them. I suppose they'll dismiss Roquefire, though he's really not to blame: in my opinion, his only fault is what he did to Saurimunda. Poor Saurimunda. There's another person I don't want to think about. At least they didn't punish her, though. At least they didn't punish her for being in the abbey compound that night.

That night . . .

"Brothers!" It's the Abbot. Oh, dear, he must have finished reading. And I didn't hear a word of it, either, though I don't suppose I missed much. I've read the Rule of Saint Benedict at least two hundred times already: in fact, I don't know why they bother reading it at all, on these occasions. No wonder it goes in one ear and out the other.

Well, in one ear and *not* out the other. Damn you, Montazin. Damn you for what you did to my ear. I don't know what you did, but you well and truly spoiled it. You've made me deaf in my left ear. Deaf, like an old man!

Or perhaps it wasn't you. Perhaps it was God's punishment. I could understand that. I deserve that; I deserve to be punished for what I did to Raymond.

"Brothers," says the Abbot, and his voice is very soft and tired, just like his face. He sits on his throne as if he belongs there; when he closes the book he doesn't pass it to Gerard, the way Guilabert always did, but holds and caresses it, absent-mindedly, like a man who really knows and loves the written word.

"Brothers," he continues, "today we welcome the novices to our chapter, and we welcome them not in Latin, which some of them don't understand, but in the language of the people. The common language."

He looks down at us, at the three of us, standing here by ourselves in the middle of the floor like pimples on a bull's backside: at Ademar, the Walking Scar; at Roland, tall and thin and beautiful; at yours truly, held together with rags and string and old bits of wood.

He smiles at us. "Today," he says, "it is my solemn duty to present three of our novices— Ademar, Roland, and Pagan—with a choice. A very important choice. Ademar, step forward, please."

Ademar steps forward. His head is bowed, his face almost hidden.

"Ademar, you have been with us now for twelve months. During that time you have submitted willingly to the excellent virtue of obedience. You have surrendered dominion over your heart and soul, and humbled yourself before the dread judgment of the Lord Christ, our true king. With a patient and quiet mind you have devoted yourself to prayer, and watched over the actions of your life every hour of the day."

A pause, as the Abbot studies Ademar with the

most intense concentration. At last he says, "Ademar, do you love the Lord God with all your heart, with all your soul, with all your strength?"

Ademar nods. "I do," he whispers. It's the first time I've heard his voice in—oh, in months. Months and months. It sounds like someone sharpening an axe on a whetstone.

"And do you desire everlasting life with your entire spiritual longing," the Abbot inquires, "to the exclusion of all else, temporal or spiritual?"

"I do."

"Ademar, in your wish to enter this holy community, the Abbey of Saint Martin, are you still steadfast of purpose?"

"I am."

"Then you are welcome." The Abbot smiles again and leans forward, as if he'd like to get up. "Today, at Mass, you will present your Act of Profession. You will be bound with the sacred and inviolable bonds of your vows, and you will join our loving brotherhood of worship. So if you go with Brother Bernard, he will take you to the sacristy, where you can prepare yourself for Mass. Brother Bernard?"

And off they trudge. One down, two to go. My heart is beating so hard that I can barely hear anything else. What a strain this is! But when the Abbot turns to Roland, his smile is very encouraging.

"Roland, step forward, please."

Roland steps forward. He doesn't look nervous: his face is a mask, his eyes blue and blank. But I know that he is nervous. I know it, because I know him. Inside and out.

"Roland, you have been with us for eight months, and during that time you have denied yourself to follow Christ." (How true.) "You have become a stranger to the ways of the world, chastising the flesh while you nurtured the spirit. Rarely have I witnessed such a profound desire to attain that love of God which casteth out fear. Roland, you have truly set your foot on God's path . . . but your journey is not yet complete."

The Abbot is still straining forward: you can tell that he doesn't want to sit on his throne. He wants to spring up and grab Roland's hand and sit down next to him. He wants to tuck his arm into Roland's and take him for a walk around the cloisters. He's speaking *to* Roland, not at him, with knitted brows and a gentle gaze and an earnest, troubled expression.

"My son," he says, "you have yet to learn the essence of our last Instrument of Good Works:

'Never despair of God's mercy.' Have you forgotten the words of Saint Paul? He said that God loveth a cheerful giver. The fruit of the Holy Spirit is joy and peace, not misery and despair. My son, you have yet to find the Holy Spirit, and without the Holy Spirit you cannot be a happy monk." Hard words, but they're softened by his smile, which is warm, sympathetic, and ever so slightly quizzical. "However," he adds, "I know that you are searching diligently, and I am anxious to help you in your search. Roland, in your wish to enter this holy community, the Abbey of Saint Martin, are you steadfast of purpose?"

Roland squares his shoulders.

"I am," he says.

"Then you will stay here for another four months, as a novice, and I will speak to you again at the end of that time."

Hooray! He's done it. Roland moves back to his seat soundlessly, and now I'm all alone, encircled by staring monks, with my arm in a sling and a crack in my head and my face a mass of bruises. Feeling very, very vulnerable.

"Pagan, step forward, please."

Stepping forward, and here I am: face to face with the Abbot. Last time I saw him was in the infirmary, with Clement, when he asked a few questions and left.

God knows what he thinks of me now.

"Pagan," he begins, and his voice has changed. But at least he's still smiling. "Pagan, it's hard for me to know what to say to you. Sometimes I feel that you have been nothing but a curse, and that's unfair because I know that what you've done, you've done for the good of Saint Martin. I also know that everyone in this room owes you the most profound debt of gratitude. That's why I would dearly love to welcome you into our community." He hesitates, sighs, bites his lip. "But I can't," he says at last.

What? What do you mean? Murmurs from the audience. Looking at Roland, who's risen to his feet again.

"I've talked about this with Brother Clement," the Abbot continues, firmly, "and we both feel that you don't really belong here. But we're not going to discuss it with you now. We'll do it after chapter."

My mind's a blank. I can't think. They're going to throw me out? Just like that? But what about Roland? What about my arm? I don't—I don't know what to do. . . .

He's rising. The Abbot's rising, and so is everyone else. Is it finished? Is it the end of chapter? It must be, I suppose, because they're all walking out. All of them except Clement. And Roland. And the Abbot, of course; he's beside me now, and his hand is on my arm.

"Come and sit down, Pagan." It's as if he's speaking from inside a well. No, not a well—don't think about wells. What am I doing? Things aren't making sense.

The Abbot's voice, close to my ear, but sounding so far away. "Sit down, Pagan. I know this is a shock."

"My lord." And that's Roland: he's stayed behind. He and Clement, but the rest of them are gone. "My lord, I must speak," he says.

"Yes, Roland?"

"My lord, if Pagan is sent away, then I must go with him."

Silence. Oh, Roland. Would you really? Oh, Roland, God bless you for that. God bless you.

But of course it's out of the question.

"Would you abandon your holy vocation for *Pagan's* sake?" Clement says sharply.

The Abbot, however, stretches out a hand. "'What man doth live without affections?'" he murmurs. "Come here, Roland. Sit down. I have to talk to you."

So here we are. The Abbot in the middle, Roland on one side, and the source of everyone's problems on the other. Feeling very small in the big, empty chapter house, which still smells of bad breath and sweaty feet. That's one thing I won't miss when I go: the concentrated smell of sweaty monastic feet. It's positively suffocating.

"Roland, Saint Augustine had much to say about love," the Abbot declares thoughtfully. "He said: 'Let the root of love be within; of this root can nothing spring but what is good.' He also said: 'Love, but take heed what you love.' My son, you have a loving heart, so you must learn to take this foundation of earthly love in your heart and build upon it a tower that will carry you to the higher love of Christ. I believe that you can build such a tower here, in this abbey."

"But—"

"With my help, Roland. With my help." The Abbot shakes his head. "I am grievously to blame for what's been happening here. I should not have been absent for so long, on so many occasions. It wasn't entirely my fault but—" He pauses; clicks his tongue; drives his fist into his knee. "No!" he says. "No, it *was* my fault. If I had been determined to stay, I would have stayed. You must forgive me, and accept my promise that in the future I shall be here, where I should be, to help you in your search for God."

Oh, yes, go right ahead. Go on and help him. But you won't help *me*, will you?

Roland stares down at his hands and swallows. "I cannot stay," he says dully. "Not if you expel Pagan."

"Roland, we're not going to throw Pagan out onto the streets. We have other plans for Pagan."

The Abbot turns, and suddenly we're eyeball to eyeball, and it's like being pinned to a wall by a lance.

"Pagan," he says, "you may not realize this, but Brother Clement is an unusually learned person. He has studied at university, and would be there still but for two reasons: first, because in 1163 the Council of Tours prohibited monks from studying law and medicine at university; second, because he believes—and I share his belief—that one of the most important tasks we have is to train and nurture our novices. Without good novices, we are nothing. So Brother Clement has devoted his life

to winnowing the grain from the chaff, and plant-
ing the grain, and watching it grow."

Really? And what's that supposed to mean? Are
you saying *I'm* the chaff? Is that what you're saying? Glaring at Clement, but he doesn't move a
muscle: just stands there, leaning on his stick, with
a grumpy expression on his face.

"After twenty-six years as a novice-master, Brother
Clement knows when a person isn't suitable for the
monastic life," the Abbot goes on. He takes my
hand, my good hand, and gives it a squeeze. He
looks deep into my eyes. "I think you know that
yourself, too." (Gently.) "Don't you, Pagan?"

The church. The music. The embrace. I remember all of that. And I remember the tears, as well; I
remember the harsh taste of them. Oh, Jesus.

"Yes." Gasp. Gulp. "Yes, my lord."

"Pagan, you simply don't have the makings of a
monk," says the Abbot. He drops my hand, glances
at Clement, takes a deep breath. "But you do have
the makings of a brilliant canon lawyer. Father
Clement says that you have one of the sharpest
and clearest intellects that he's ever come across.
He says he's never met anyone of your age who's
so quick, or so able, with such an extraordinary

grasp of ideas and their practical application. He says he's neglected the other novices for your sake, so that he could give you the kind of attention you needed. But he's gone as far as he can. That's why he wants to send you to Carcassonne, to the cathedral school.

"From there, you will have a chance of reaching university."

What? I don't—what was that? Is this some kind of joke? But the Abbot seems quite serious. And Clement—Clement's just standing there, leaning on his stick. Staring at the floor.

He won't even look at me.

"The Bishop of Carcassonne is my cousin," the Abbot explains. "I will ask him to accept you into the cathedral chapter, as a secondary. I think the life of a secular canon will suit you much better than the life of a monk. It's a freer life, and it's concerned with the world. We are concerned only with God. Although, of course, we are all serving God in our different ways." He turns back to Roland. "Knowing this, Roland—knowing that your dear friend will be safe and cared for—will you consent to stay here with us?"

Roland lifts his head. He looks at me with his blue eyes, and they're solemn and questioning, and of course he has to stay, he *has* to stay now that the Abbot's back, because if he leaves this place, he'll never be happy: he'll never be at peace. And if Roland isn't happy, I'll never be happy either.

Go on, Roland. It's all right, I swear. There's only one choice for you—one choice and one path. You have to take it.

Please.

"Very well," he says at last. "Very well, my lord, I'll stay." And he leans back, sighing like a man who's just finished the most exhausting race of his life.

CHAPTER THIRTY-ONE

Isn't it odd how much better a place looks when you're leaving it? Even this dormitory looks cozier, somehow. Even my bed . . . just think, I've been sleeping in this bed for longer than I've slept in any bed since I was ten years old, and I'll never sleep in it again. Never. Last night was the last time.

"Carcassonne isn't far," says Roland, breaking the silence. "It's less than half a day's ride from Saint Martin's."

"Mmmm."

Pause. He's sitting on the bed opposite, watching me dress. My old tunic, so stained and shabby. My old stockings. My old cloak, smelling of herbs. They must have stored it with herbs, to stop insects from chewing holes in the fabric.

It's so hard to get dressed when I can't use my arm.

"Here," says Roland, rising to his feet. "I'm sorry. I'll help you."

He undoes the knot in my girdle and pulls my robe over my head, carefully, because there are scabs it might catch on. When he picks up my tunic he holds it for a moment, staring at the ancient brown bloodstains on the hem.

"You can write to me," he mutters. "I can always ask someone to read it. I can always ask someone to write a reply."

Oh, sure. That'll be something to look forward to. Pushing my arms through the sleeves of my tunic, but the sleeves are too narrow for the splint.

"We'll have to tear it," Roland decides, and rips the worn fabric right up to the elbow. Never mind. Who cares? I'll only be wearing this sad old thing until I reach the cathedral. Then I suppose they'll put me into something else. Anyway, it doesn't even fit anymore: it seems a little short. A little tight.

"You've grown," says Roland. "You've filled out."

He picks up my belt and fastens it around my waist. Picks up my sword, in its dangling scabbard.

Will I be needing that?

"Take it," he says. "You still have to reach Carcassonne."

True. Very true. My stockings feel damp: they need a good airing. My old boots look exactly like a pair of mummified eels. One more trip for these old campaigners, and then they ought to be given a proper burial. Roland actually smiles when he sees them.

"They've covered a lot of ground," he begins, and suddenly seems to lose his voice.

Don't, Roland. Just don't.

He arranges the cloak around my shoulders, and I'm ready. Ready? What a joke. This is—I think I'm going to die. I'm going to walk out that door and die.

"Come on," he says. And now I've left the dormitory, never to return. Walking along the path to the herb-garden wall. The sky's still pink; there's still dew on the grass. And there's a group of people waiting under the olive tree.

Are they here for my sake? I suppose they are. Durand's crying; his nose is running; he looks terrible. He darts forward—hugging me—and I can feel his tears on my neck.

"I'll miss you," he sobs. "I'll miss you, Pagan."

Oh, God. How can this be happening? And Gaubert, little Gaubert. I have to bend over to embrace him. He feels so delicate, like a bird.

"Goodbye, Pagan." His voice quavers. "Come back soon."

I think I'm going to break, but no—no, I'm not. Because here's Bernard, and he hates me now; he blames me for everything that happened to Raymond. He can't even bring himself to touch me.

"Goodbye," he says. And good riddance: the unspoken words are clear in his eyes.

Forgive me, Bernard. Forgive me for what I've done to you.

"Take care of yourself." It's Amiel. Exhausted, ghostly, his touch as weak as a butterfly's. This may be the last time I see him; he may not live much longer. But what can I say? If I speak, it will be the end. I'll be finished. And I can't risk that.

Moving from Amiel to Gaucher. Never liked Gaucher. Glad to see the back of him. Perfunctory hug . . . and here's Ademar. Ademar? It can't be. Stopping to stare at him. He stares right back. Doesn't have to say or do anything. Just the fact that he's come—I still don't believe it.

And Clement's next in line.

Clement, leaning against the olive tree. (He's propped his stick against the wall.) But he pushes himself upright and takes a step forward. Holds out his arms. I can see over his shoulder; I can feel his bones grinding as he squeezes, as he staggers, using my weight to support himself. His harsh breathing. His voice in my ear—my right ear.

"Make me proud," he mumbles. "Make me even prouder." He pulls back, and raises his clumsy, swollen hands until I can feel them on my face, one on each cheek, and he bends down and kisses my forehead. Kisses it hard.

Sweet Jesus.

The tears; they're coming. I can't stop them now. I can't see and I can't breathe, and if I breathe, I'll howl. I'll collapse. Someone's hand on my arm. "Come on, Pagan." How can this be happening? How did I get all these friends? And Clement— Clement never told me—

Through a door. Gravel underfoot. Stables and horses, three horses, and the Abbot's on one of them, dressed for riding. Good horses. Big horses. The second one's a bay gelding, with a servant in the saddle.

The third one must be mine.

"Pagan?" It's Roland's voice. No, I can't. I can't leave him.

"I can't leave you . . ."

Bawling like a baby. God, oh, God, this is unbearable. But he's still there, all warm and solid, his arms and his chest and his back, stooping now, so he can lay his cheek against my head. So I can lay my head against his heart. Holding him tight, because soon I'll be gone.

Roland. My mother and my father. My friend. My lord.

Help me. Please help me to leave you.

"You'll be all right," he says softly.

"I can't—I can't—"

"Yes, you can. You can do anything. Everything." He swallows; I can feel it shuddering down his throat and into his chest. "Don't make this any harder, Pagan, please. The Abbot is waiting."

The Abbot. Yes. The Abbot is waiting. Can't let the Abbot wait. Releasing my grip; turning blindly toward where the horses were, before I drowned them in a flood of tears. No—hold on—I can see them again. And I can see the Abbot, too: he's gazing politely off into the distance.

While his servant gawks at us like an owl.

"I'll help you up," says Roland.

Owl Eyes is holding my horse, but he surrenders the reins to Roland, who flicks them back over the long, snowy neck, where they're supposed to be.

"Put your arm across my shoulders, Pagan, and I'll lift you. No—no, put your foot there. That's it. That's right. Be careful. Good."

A struggle, a stagger, a jerk of the reins. And suddenly I'm up. I'm up! Now I just have to ride the damned thing.

How long has it been since I sat on a horse?

"This is an extremely placid animal," the Abbot assures me. He looks very organized: riding gloves, riding hoots, saddlebags with his initials on them. "Even one-handed, you'll be able to ride her. All she does is follow the horse in front." He glances at Roland, grimaces, and turns away. "We have to go now," he says.

Owl Eyes clicks his tongue. The Abbot digs in his heels. They're both moving. They're both going.

Roland is still holding my reins.

"Roland—"

"Pray for me. Think of me." He grabs my good hand and presses it to his lips. He folds my fingers around the reins. He steps back. "I'll see you again," he says, and slaps the white crupper in front of him.

With a snort and a shiver, my horse begins to move. It begins to follow the big, brown backside in front of it, heading for the abbey gates. It feels so peculiar. So high and unsteady and—and—

Twisting in my saddle, but Roland's already turned his back. He's turned his back, and he's walking toward the herb-garden wall. No, he's not going in there. He's going somewhere else. Why doesn't he look? Why doesn't he wave? But before we turn the corner, I can see him stop.

He stops, and covers his face with his hand.

Oh, Roland. Oh, Roland. Now he's out of sight, and we're passing the dormitory. Passing the guest-house. Coming up to the gates. The gates! Watching the porter, as he lifts his hand to us. Under the archway, from shadow into sunlight.

Through the gates.

I'm through the gates now. I've left them behind. I'm outside the abbey, for the first time in eight months: there are the fields, and the trees, and the road unrolling before me. And there, near the wall, sitting on a rock—it's Saurimunda.

She looks up. Her mouth drops open. She scrambles to her feet and stretches out her hands, but I'm already passing. I can't stop; I can't help. I can't even smile, because her face is breaking my heart.

Straining back over my shoulder, to watch her receding form. A drab little patch against the stonework. Beside her, the solid, gray weight of the gatehouse, with its tiny windows and its crenelated towers. And its cross. And its carvings.

And its massive wooden gates, slowly shutting behind me.